DOUBLE DANGER

Other B&W titles
by Margaret Thomson Davis

THE BREADMAKER'S SAGA
THE NEW BREADMAKERS
THE CLYDESIDERS TRILOGY
THE TOBACCO LORDS TRILOGY
A DARKENING OF THE HEART
THE DARK SIDE OF PLEASURE
BURNING AMBITION
THE GLASGOW BELLE
LIGHT AND DARK
WRITE FROM THE HEART
A DEADLY DECEPTION
GOODMANS OF GLASSFORD STREET
RED ALERT

MARGARET THOMSON
DAVIS

DOUBLE
DANGER

B & W PUBLISHING

First published 2009
by Black & White Publishing Ltd
29 Ocean Drive, Edinburgh EH6 6JL

1 3 5 7 9 10 8 6 4 2 0 9 10 11 12

ISBN: 978 1 84502 265 5

Copyright © Margaret Thomson Davis 2009

Typeset by RefineCatch Ltd, Bungay, Suffolk

Printed and bound by MPG Books Ltd

ACKNOWLEDGEMENTS

I would like to thank Margot and Evelyn Cook, Margaret Martin and Debbie Healy for their generous help with my Barras research. Many thanks also to Evelyn Pullar and Edward Finnigan for their detailed information about life in Saudi Arabia and Dubai.

Librarians have always been kind and helpful to me but none more so than the librarians at Bishopbriggs Library while I was working on *Double Danger*.

The latter part of the book is set in the Campsie Hills area. However, no such place as Vale of Lennox exists. And Hilltop House is an imaginative mixture of several locations from different areas across Scotland.

DEDICATION

This book is dedicated with gratitude and admiration to Edward Finnigan and his mother Evelyn Pullar.

I

Saudi Arabia – Jessica McKay had never heard of it until she met Brian Anderson. She was working as usual at the Barras market stall owned by Mrs Margaret Mellors. Then along comes this gorgeous man with blue-black hair and a deep tan. Her own hair was what she regarded as boring brown, and long and outrageously thick and curly. The only way she could tame it was by tying it back, but a thick crowd of curls still escaped and bunched over her forehead.

The man poked curiously around all the goods on the stall.

'Can I help you?' she asked.

He just smiled and said, 'I'm only having a look around.'

'That's a great tan you've got. Been away on holiday?'

'No, I work in Saudi Arabia.'

'Saudi Arabia?' Jessica echoed incredulously.

'In a compound in the desert. I'm Brian Anderson, by the way.'

'Gosh!'

'When we lived in Bishopbriggs, my father once took me with him to visit the Barras. I was quite small at the time and I don't remember all that much about it. Then we moved to Bearsden and I went to school there until I got a place at Dundee University. After my parents died, I'd nothing to come back to Bearsden or Glasgow for.'

Jessica stretched out her hand.

'Jessica McKay.' Mrs Mellors and everyone at the Barras called her Jessie, but she felt that Jessica would sound better to Brian Anderson.

Her hand tingled as it was gripped by his. She felt quite excited, but of course she always had been an excitable person.

'Don't tell me you came all the way from a compound in the desert just for a look around the Barras!'

He laughed.

'No. But we all get so fed up with Arab food. Most of us come over occasionally to stock up with things like Marmite and Vegemite and sauces and herbs.'

'Marmite?' She sounded incredulous.

'Oh yes, you get that you long for the sight of a pot of good old Marmite.'

Against the deep tan of his skin, his teeth were startling white. She'd never seen such a handsome man in her life.

'What's a compound?' she asked. 'Is it mostly Arabs who live there?'

'It's a good mile square with high walls and guards at different points. Inside, it's really beautiful with well-kept gardens and villas and every amenity, like a swimming pool, a medical centre, a leisure centre, a restaurant, a golf club, a café and so on. It's mostly Scots and English who live in the compound. The gardens are beautifully maintained by the south-east Asian and Indian workers. We get hot summers and mild winters and rain usually from November to March, so that helps the gardens.'

'But it's an Arab country?'

'Oh yes, we do business with them and I find they are mostly hospitable and friendly. But their customs take a bit of getting used to.'

'How do you mean?'

A couple of customers interrupted her at this point and she had to reluctantly attend to them.

2

'When do you knock off?' he asked.

She glanced at her watch. 'Mrs Mellors is due any minute. She's been away having her tea and I'll get time off for mine when she gets back. Here she is now.'

'Can I take you for a meal? I'm enjoying our chat.'

'Thanks. So am I.'

She immediately lifted her coat and struggled into it. Mrs Mellors, a small slim perky woman, grinned at her.

'You're in a great hurry today, hen.'

'This is Brian Anderson, Mrs Mellors. He's invited me out for tea.'

'Oh aye? Well.' She turned to Brian. 'You look after her, do you hear me, and bring her back here safe and sound.'

Brian gave a mock salute. 'Your wish is my command.'

'We'd better just go somewhere nearby,' Jessica told him, 'since there's not much time. A snack in one of the bars would do me OK.'

'All right,' he said.

They went across to Bar 67 which was comparatively quiet as there was no football match on. It was called Bar 67 because Celtic won the European cup in 1967, the first British team ever to win it.

'So you get on OK with the Arabs then?' Jessica asked after they'd settled down with a drink and some food.

'Well, their customs take a bit of getting used to, as I said. There's a lot of touching and close contact. Arab men walk hand in hand, for instance.'

'Gosh. Does that mean they're all . . .'

'No, no, far from it. No, it's just the custom. They're even liable to take a Western man's hand as they walk along with him.'

Jessica was fascinated. She'd never heard the like of it in her life.

'It can be infuriating to have a business appointment with them, as I often need to. It's supposed to be a private appointment but it's always interrupted by phone calls and visits from their friends and family.'

'No!'

'Oh yes, even at the best of times business meetings are much slower and start with long enquiries into one's health and journey. It's really maddening but you've to be careful never to show any annoyance or impatience.'

The time flew by and eventually Jessica said, 'I'd better go. Thanks for everything. I've really enjoyed talking to you.'

'Can I keep seeing you while I'm here? I've made no plans for my leave, other than the shopping, and I've done all that today. I've rented a serviced apartment nearby so it's no problem to call for you. You don't work in the Barras during the week, do you? The market's just open at weekends, if I remember.'

'Yes, OK.'

'Where do you live? I could call for you tomorrow first thing and we could tour around Glasgow. It feels like it's a lifetime since I've been to the old place. I'd really enjoy touring around everywhere.' He flashed her one of his smiles. 'Especially with such good company.'

They made their way back across the road.

'You'll see an awful lot of changes. That's where I live – above the market.'

'272A The Gallowgate,' he said. 'I'll remember that and call for you at – what, nine o'clock?'

'Fine, see you then.' She ran back into the market, eager to tell Mrs Mellors all about her new friend.

'You watch yourself,' Margaret Mellors warned her. 'He's a right man of the world and you're just a wee lassie. You've only got me to see to you. I'm lucky, I've got a marvellous son. He'd do anything for me.'

'I know. I know. But it'll be great. We can maybe walk in the direction of the Trongate first. I know my Glasgow history.

History was my favourite subject at school. All around there and right up the High Street is the oldest area of Glasgow.'

'What's wrong with starting here and telling him all about the Barras? I bet even you didn't know that this is the largest enclosed market in Europe. There's thousands of traders, not to mention the hundreds of shopkeepers spilling out into the streets all around.'

'I did know but he's had a look around here already today. He told me how he was admiring the big decorative gates, as he called them. He was down here early this morning having a walk around all the stalls.'

'He couldn't have got round them all.'

'Well, some. Anyway, I think he's absolutely wonderful.'

'Aye, I can see that but just you remember what I've said – watch yourself.'

'All right, all right.'

After she finished work, she ran up the stairs to her flat.

She was lucky to have such a lovely big place – three bedrooms it had, and a nice big sitting room, a kitchen and a bathroom. And no flats above her. Her parents had invested all the money from their stall in the house – had bought everything outright, and so now she was living rent-free.

Happily Jessica went over to the kitchen window, opened it and rested her elbows on the sill. Down below and all around as far as the eye could see were the brilliant, multi-coloured booths, trading carts, barrows and tables all laid out under the corrugated iron canopy. Absolutely everything you could think of was sold here, including the kitchen sink. And the noise was ear-splitting. The vendors were vying with one another in boasting about their wares and what marvellous bargains they were offering.

One wee woman was yelling, 'Epples, a tanner each. No, I kid ye not. These epples are only a tanner each.'

A man was juggling plates and bawling, 'I'm not asking you for £30 for these beautiful plates, not even £20. No, believe it or not, not even £10. Come up quick enough and you can have them for £3 each. Yes folks, I swear it, if you're quick enough, I'll let them go for just £3 each.'

Jessica chuckled to herself. He had probably paid fifty pence each for them. She felt part of the huge crowd and crescendo of noise and she clapped her hands in excitement and delight.

There were lots of Cockney accents to be heard. Quite a few men came up with packed vans from London and got to like the Barras so much that they bought houses in Glasgow and made it their home base. They never lost their Cockney accents, though, or their Cockney humour. The Cockneys had some of the best patter in the market and created the loudest laughs.

Eventually Jessica shut the window and went through to the bedroom to study herself in the wardrobe mirror. She could hardly believe her luck that such a handsome and fascinating man wanted to spend the next three or four weeks with her. After all, she was no raving beauty. OK, she was slim and quite shapely but what an enormous, curly mop of hair she had hanging right down her back. It was as thick as a bush and made her look crazy if she let it hang loose.

There was nothing she could do to tame it, except tie it back. Nothing at all, though, to keep the bundle of curls from sticking over her brow. She looked eccentric, to say the least. Brian Anderson must have liked her, though, to want to spend the whole of his leave with her. It was amazing and exciting and wonderful. She danced around the room and then flung herself recklessly on to the bed and kicked her heels.

2

Dead on nine o'clock next morning, the doorbell rang and there he was, dressed in a dark suit, pale blue shirt and silver tie.

He had a bag slung over his shoulder. He patted it.

'Got a plastic raincoat and a camera, a notebook and a tape recorder in here.'

'Gosh, you're well organised. Come in for a minute while I get my jacket.'

How she wished now that she'd put on something smarter than her white trainers, blue denims and white polo neck. It had been showery earlier and she'd thought if they were going to be traipsing around outside for hours on end, it would be more sensible to wear casual clothes. Her jacket was waterproof and had a hood.

'This is a lovely big flat,' he said, staring around. 'I bet you don't often see high corniced ceilings like that nowadays.'

'My mother and father bought the flat with money they earned at their stall.'

'Oh, so they were market people?'

'Yes, and I used to help them when I was wee. I ran around collecting the money and handing it up to them.'

'What did you sell?'

'Oh, lots of different things over the years. Dolls, handbags, canteens of cutlery, tea sets, jewellery. For a while, they went in for curtains and my father was called the curtain man. But I remember the dolls best. He'd pay about 25 shillings each for dolls and then sell them for £3, even £5 for a bigger doll.'

'You're not old enough to remember shillings and pence.'

They left the flat and she turned the key in the lock.

'As I said, I was just a wee girl when I worked for them but my mother used to tell me things. We had many a good laugh, my mother and me.'

Out on the street, Jessica said, 'Will we start here – I mean, will I tell you something about how the market started?'

Already she was beginning to feel a bit disturbed and fluttery. It was the way he was looking at her. It was difficult to concentrate on ancient history when the present was so close and pulsatingly vivid.

'It was started in the early twenties by a woman called Maggie McIver. At thirteen, she was asked to look after a Parkhead vendor's barrow and found that she was more successful than he was.'

'At thirteen?' Brian said. 'That's amazing.'

'Within the year, she had a barrow of her own. Soon she married a fellow barrow trader called Samuel McIver and bought land and created a permanent market site. A folk singer called Matt McGinn belonged around here and knew the Barras well.' She giggled and burst into one of his humorous songs.

Brian laughed and suddenly tucked her arm through his. 'A good singer as well. Is there no end to your talents?'

She felt herself blush but pushed on.

'There's what was once the Barrowland Ballroom. Maggie McIver used to give all the hawkers a free meal with a drink and a dance at Christmas, but one year she couldn't get the hall she wanted. So she built her own and called it the Barrowland Dance Hall.'

'Quite a woman.'

'Oh definitely.'

'I wonder if Charles Dickens met her. Maybe his visit would be too early but he must have met people like her. He was so enthusiastic about the place. He said of his visit to Glasgow, "I have never been more heartily received anywhere or enjoyed myself more completely." '

'That's the best of having been to university,' Jessica said. 'You learn things like that.'

'Oh, believe me, you're exceptionally knowledgeable, Jessica, without any university education.'

'I know a lot about Glasgow, right enough. I don't think there's a corner of it I don't know about and haven't been to. And of course they all know me at the library. I read every book I can find about Glasgow. The librarians keep aside any new books for me and let me have them when I go in. I spend a lot of my free time in the library. Or just wandering around all the streets.'

'Well, I've been really lucky meeting you, Jessica. I couldn't have found a better guide.'

He squeezed her arm against his chest and smiled down at her. She prayed he wouldn't feel her fast-racing pulse. To help ignore the turmoil of her emotions, she burst into speech again.

'Talking of Dickens, or at least of his time, the Saracen Head pub, or the Sarry Heid as it's best known, dates back to the eighteenth century. It's all dark and wood-panelled inside, and Black Angus – I think he's still the owner – gives out whisky for next to nothing from a studio round the corner to tramps, thieves, hawkers, writers, poets and artists. Robert Burns visited Bridgeton and stayed at the Saracen Head Inn. So did Bothwell and Johnson on their way back from their Hebridean tour.'

'How fascinating!'

'Back that way is Parkhead, where Celtic football team play. This is a great Celtic area. I suppose you'll know all about the terrible rivalry between Rangers and Celtic.' She giggled. 'There's an old Glasgow joke about a Rangers supporter who was having a terrible argument with his wife and she accused him of loving Rangers more than he loved her. "Rangers?" the man bawled. "I love Celtic more than I love you!" '

Brian gave a roar of laughter. 'I must remember that one for the lads back at the compound.'

'My boss, Margaret Mellors, is unusual. She likes both Celtic and Rangers. She goes to lots of their matches.'

'My God – at her age?'

'I don't know what age she is. She's widow with a son and three grandchildren, right enough. She loves them to bits and her son, of course. She's lucky there. He's a nice man. He makes a good living and would never see her short of a bob or two. But she's very independent. "I make my own good living," she always says. "I don't need any handouts." But she tells me that her family are planning to emigrate to Australia soon and they're trying to persuade her to go with them. There's a great opportunity to expand his business out there apparently. Mrs Mellors is trying to persuade them to go without her. She's promised she'll join them later – I hope she means much, much later.'

'She sounds a real feisty old girl. Is her flat in the same building as yours?'

'Oh no. Like a lot of people who work in Glasgow, she lives in one of the villages in the Campsie Hills area. She took me out to her nice wee cottage one day during the week for tea and brought me all the way back home again. Of course, it's only about half an hour or so from Glasgow to lots of country areas. Glasgow's very well placed that way. Her family live near her out there and her son visits her nearly every day. The way she talks about that son of hers, you'd think he was a saint.'

'You're quite happy in your flat above the market, though?'

'Oh yes, I love it. All the bustle and noise and so many people crowding about. I'd be bored to tears and restless out in Vale of Lennox. That's the village where Mrs Mellors lives. It's a nice wee cottage she's got, though, and she likes it. Lots of her Glasgow friends live there, as well as her son.'

'Well, of course, if her friends and family are nearby.'

'Will we go up the High Street?' Jessica asked. 'And then on to Castle Street? That's the oldest part of the city. There's the Cathedral and the Necropolis and the Royal Infirmary, and across the road, the oldest house in the city. It's called Provand's Lordship. A lot of famous people stayed there, including Mary Queen of Scots.'

'As long as you're not getting too tired.'

'No, I'm OK.'

'We'll stop for lunch soon.'

'Yes, OK. The first thing I think about Provand's Lordship is that at different times, it was an ale house, a sweet shop and a cabinet maker's place. Now it's a museum.'

'Will we be able to go in and have a look around?'

'Oh yes. By the way, there's a bronze statue of a horse on top of an eight-foot plinth in a wee park between the church and the High Street and it's the only bronze statue in the world with a movable plinth. In a strong wind, the horse wags its tail.'

Brian laughed. 'You're joking!'

'No, honestly. Its tail really does move. I've seen it.'

'I'll believe that when I see it.'

'The High Court is up there. That's where the last public hanging was done. He was an English doctor called Pritchard. A huge crowd apparently came to see him being hanged for poisoning his wife and his mother-in-law.'

When they reached the Trongate and Argyle Street, Brian suggested relaxing over a meal before they walked any further.

They found a restaurant and settled together in a quiet corner. For a moment, he stared at her and when she was about to burst into speech again, he placed a gentle finger on her mouth.

'Ssh. I just want to look at you for a minute.'

After he took his hand away, she said miserably,

'I've been talking far too much. I've been a right bore.'

'No, you have not. You definitely have not been boring me. I'm loving every minute of your company. You're a fascinating person to be with – full of energy, and knowledge, and passion.'

Well, he was right about the passion, she thought. But she had never felt passionate before she'd met him.

She tried to keep quiet over the meal and he did not speak much either. He smiled at her, though, and when his dark eyes met hers, the feelings she thought she saw in them made her cheeks burn.

She remembered the warning Mrs Mellors had given her.

'He's a man of the world and you're just a wee lassie.'

She had a moment's panic. She even wished Mrs Mellors was there with her, by her side now, making her feel protected and safe, as she always did. Mrs Mellors had been like a mother to her since her own mother had died.

But the moment passed and they began to talk again and she felt lucky and happy and excited again. Lucky to have such a handsome man of the world interested in her and admiring her. Excited to think of what might happen between them.

3

Jessica was engulfed in a dark strength. His weight was on top of her. His electricity was inside her. She felt dizzy. She trembled violently. She had never felt so wildly happy. Eventually he rolled away from her.

'There's someone at your door,' he said.

She'd never heard a sound.

Hastily she scrambled up. She was still fully dressed except for her knickers. He got up too as she made her way from the bedroom door and then out to the lobby.

Mrs Mellors stood on the doorstep.

'Are you all right, Jessie?'

'Yes, fine thanks.'

'You're all red and trembling. You don't look all right. Can I come in?'

Reluctantly Jessica stood aside and allowed the older woman to enter. They arrived in the kitchen to find Brian Anderson switching on the electric kettle.

'I thought a cup of tea was in order.'

'Oh yes, thanks,' Jessica said. 'I could do with one.'

'Why? What have you been up to?' Mrs Mellors asked.

But Brian answered, 'She's a big girl now.'

'No, she is not. She's just an innocent wee lassie.'

'I'm fine. Honestly. Are you staying for a cup of tea?'

'Aye, just to make sure.'

'Make sure of what?'

'I'd better go,' Brian said.

'Oh!' Jessica was deflated. She knew it couldn't last. 'Right. I'll see you to the door.'

At the outside door, he gathered her into his arms, kissed her gently, then said, 'I'll pick you up tomorrow at the same time.'

She immediately brightened.

'OK, great!'

Back in the kitchen, Mrs Mellors was filling the teapot. Jessica danced around the table, her long mop of hair bouncing and jazzing about.

'Sit down,' Mrs Mellors commanded. 'I knew that fella wouldn't do you any good.'

Jessica burst into song. 'I feel happy, oh so happy . . .'

'I don't suppose it has occurred to you for one second that after he got his wicked way with you, he'd disappear off to Saudi Arabia and that's the last you'd ever see of him. He just wants to pass his time with somebody while he's here. Make use of them like he's making use of you.'

'Och, Mrs Mellors, there's no harm done.'

'You think so? Did either of you use contraceptives?'

Jessica fell silent. In all the excitement, she hadn't remembered about that.

'I thought not. Now you could be left on your own and pregnant.'

Jessica thanked God for Mrs Mellors. She'd never be alone as long as she had her.

'He's coming for me tomorrow again. I expect he'll see me all the time he's here on leave. We didn't get time to go up the High Street and Castle Street yesterday.' She sighed with pleasure. 'We got talking. Oh, Mrs Mellors, he's really an awful nice man. I don't believe he'd want to do me any harm.'

'You wouldn't believe anything bad about anybody. You're a right wee softie. And he's seen that. He's no' daft.' She poured the tea. 'Drink that. It'll calm you down.'

'Is it so wrong to feel happy?'

'No, Jessie, it's no' wrong to feel happy.'

'Well then.'

'Just don't expect too much and don't expect it to last forever.'

'No, I won't. I promise.'

But she secretly wanted it to last forever. She prayed, fervently prayed, that it would last forever. She wanted to dance madly around the room again but managed to control the urge for Mrs Mellors' sake. With an almost superhuman effort, she remained sitting, eyes lowered, sipping tea.

Next day, at nine o'clock on the dot, the doorbell rang and as soon as she opened the door, Brian took her in his arms and gave her a long kiss.

'I'm all ready to go,' she said eventually, breathlessly. 'I see you've got your man bag ready too.'

She didn't ask him in and they proceeded arm-in-arm down the stairs. This time they strode along at a good pace, and this time didn't stop so early for lunch. They turned up the High Street and went into the oldest house in Glasgow, Provand's Lordship.

'Look at how tiny the rooms are,' Jessica said. 'Isn't it amazing to think that anyone, far less Mary Queen of Scots, could stay in a wee place like this?'

Soon they were standing back from the road gazing at the gothic Cathedral.

'It gives me the shivers,' Jessica said, 'when I think of all the poor people burned in front of that place. By one of the bishops, too. It's enough to put you off religion.'

'I know. There's been so much death and cruelty and wars all down through the ages in the name of religion.'

'What has it all got to do with gentle Jesus who preached turn the other cheek and love your neighbour?'

'I've often asked myself that.'

Next to the Cathedral but fronting the street was the huge Royal Infirmary.

Brian said, 'Now, I know about what happened in there. That's one bit of Glasgow history I did learn at university. Joseph Lister introduced an antiseptic system that revolutionised surgery. The United States ambassador to Britain said at the time, "My Lord, it is not a profession, it is not a nation, it is humanity itself which, with uncovered head, salutes you." '

'That's right. I read that in one of the books about Glasgow I got in the library,' Jessica said.

'Good for you. You see, you didn't need to go to any university. You've had an excellent education and you did it all by yourself.'

Suddenly he put out a hand to hail a passing taxi.

'Let's go into the centre – George Square, perhaps. Time for a seat and a coffee.'

'Great. There's lots I can tell you about George Square. There's a hotel there with a tea area and a whole wall of windows that look out directly on to the square.'

Within minutes, the taxi had dropped them off at the hotel next to Queen Street railway station. They went into the hotel and found a seat in the glass-fronted area where there was a tea and coffee bar.

Again Jessica trembled at Brian's gaze. He seemed to be staring into her soul, searching out everything about her.

'You're making me blush,' she laughed, 'staring at me like that.'

'I want to find out everything about you. Really get to know you before I have to go back to Saudi. There's so little time.'

'Oh!' She felt suddenly miserable. 'I keep forgetting. You're just here for a wee while.'

The waiter came with their coffee and for a few minutes they both sipped the steaming liquid in silence. Then Jessica rushed into reckless speech.

'The City Chambers over on your left is a magnificent building, outside and inside. It's got the most beautiful Italian marble floors and staircase. The view from the first landing is truly magnificent. We must go on one of the tours.' She paused for breath before rattling on under his steady gaze. 'There's tier upon tier of pillars and arches and there's a vast conical ceiling in richly ornamented plasterwork and a cupola filled with tinted glass, to mention but a few things!'

'Sounds beautiful.'

'Oh it is. It really is. All of the rooms are. But the most beautiful room is the huge banqueting hall with its arched ceiling and paintings all round depicting scenes from the history of the city. And gosh, you should see the chandeliers.'

'We'll perhaps have time for a tour another day. In the meantime, drink up your coffee.'

'I'm talking too much,' she said.

'I've asked you to tell me all about the city and I'm interested. I feel ashamed that I've lived so long in Dundee and now abroad and completely lost touch with Glasgow. You're doing me a favour, Jessica, and I appreciate it.' He sipped his coffee before adding, 'And I admire your knowledge of the city.'

'I love the place,' she admitted. 'Always have.'

'You could easily get a job as a tourist guide.'

'Och no, I'm too happy at the Barras working for Mrs Mellors. I love that place best of all and my lovely flat looking down on it – it's part of the market, really.'

'You wouldn't want to live anywhere else?'

'Oh no, definitely not.'

She wondered if she'd said something wrong.

He sighed and a sad expression clouded his eyes. Then he shrugged. 'Right. Where to next, my excellent tour guide?'

17

'Buchanan Street perhaps, but before we leave here, have a look at the statues – eleven of them, with Sir Walter Scott the highest. That always annoys me. Why should he be the highest and look the important one above Robert Burns? The citizens of Glasgow had to donate enough money to have the one of Burns erected, otherwise there would have been nothing to him at all.'

'You're a fan of Robert Burns then?'

'Oh yes, definitely. I can recite lots of his poems. I've a great memory.'

He smiled. 'Yes, I've gathered that.'

They finished their coffee and made their way first of all along to the Gallery of Modern Art, outside of which, high on a plinth, was a statue of the Duke of Wellington seated on his horse. No matter how often officials removed the red traffic cone perched rakishly on his head, some witty and agile Glaswegian climbed up and put it back again.

Jessica was used to seeing it and didn't remark on it but Brian burst into hearty laughter.

'Isn't that so typical of the true Glaswegian.'

She wasn't quite sure what he meant but she enjoyed the affectionate hug he gave her. Indeed, she felt light-headed with passion. She could hardly wait for night to come.

4

'Can I be completely honest with you, Jessica?' Brian asked.

'Sure.'

'I don't know why you prefer to live in the Calton rather than in a better area. You do have a lovely flat. Is it really the flat that keeps you here?'

'No, I told you before. I love the place. Everything about it, and I especially love working in the Barras. Mrs Mellors has often tried to get me to give up this flat – rent it out maybe – and get a cottage near her in Vale of Lennox.'

'And you refused to go and live in such a lovely place? I remember going for walks and hill-climbing in the Campsies while I was at school in Bearsden.'

'I know it might sound crazy.'

'It does. Mrs Mellors could have given you a lift to and from work in the Barras, if you still wanted to work there.'

'I know. But I love being part of the place. I often open my back window and lean out and I can see the market and feel a real part of it – the noise, the dirt, the smell, as it says in the song. It's all so exciting. And all my memories are here. I was working at my mum and dad's stall when I was only a primary school kid. I was even toddling around the stall before that. It's in my blood, I suppose. It's me.'

He sighed.

'I can see it excites you, right enough.'

'It has such an interesting history too. Remember the Saracen's Head Inn I showed you yesterday? On display inside is a blunderbuss carried for protection on the London coach. And a skull found during digging operations on the site. The spot the inn was built on, you see, was once the Kirkyard of Little St Mungo's Chapel, where lepers were buried.'

'God, they built a pub and a hotel on top of a lepers' burial place? I suppose the graves were converted into wine cellars and kitchens.'

'Yes,' she giggled. 'Could be.'

Brian rolled his eyes. 'I don't think I'll be going there for a meal.'

'Och, there won't be any danger of catching leprosy after all this time.'

'All the same, the mere idea of what's down there would be enough to put me off my food.'

They were sitting having afternoon tea in the Willow Tearoom above a jeweller's shop in Sauchiehall Street. The tearoom was to a design by Charles Rennie Mackintosh, the world-famous Glasgow architect.

'Anyway, the chairs in the Saracen's Head are more comfortable than these high-backed things,' Jessica said. 'OK, they look different from any other chairs and are elegant too, but I don't think he ever thought of comfort when he designed all his furniture. Did you like his design of the Glasgow School of Art?' she asked.

'Yes, but I was surprised at how scruffy and dirty it looked. Tourists must come from all over the world to look at that. As you say, he is world-famous.'

'But it's a working place. Students work there every day and go in and out all the time.'

'Yes, that would explain it. But I still think they ought to employ more cleaners.'

'Must be lack of cash.'

He smiled. 'You won't tolerate even the slightest criticism of your native city, will you?'

'Oh, I don't think that's true. Well, maybe not of the Calton, right enough.'

He shook his head in disbelief. 'The Calton's perfect as it is?'

'To me it is.'

'Can I stay with you in your perfect flat tonight?'

'OK, great!'

It had been great every night they had spent together so far. Despite Mrs Mellors' warnings, she had continued to have a truly wonderful time and no matter what happened, no matter that any day now he'd be leaving for a far-off country, she'd still feel everything had been worth it. She had not, and was sure she would never have, any regrets.

After leaving the Willow Tearoom, they walked up Sauchiehall Street, past Charing Cross to the huge Mitchell Library. She'd heard that this building held the biggest collection of archives and reference books in Europe. Certainly the Burns Room and the Glasgow Room had been favourite haunts of hers for years. They spent some time in both rooms before returning to Sauchiehall Street. Off Sauchiehall Street in Elmbank Street was the King's Theatre, and Brian went and booked a couple of seats for the next evening's musical.

'If it's all right with you, we can have dinner, then go to the show to celebrate my last evening of my leave here. I've promised to stay for a few days with an Arab friend in his flat in Dubai before going back to Saudi. Have you ever seen pictures of Dubai?'

She wasn't in the slightest interested in Dubai. She felt suddenly and completely shattered at his imminent departure. No doubt he'd told her at some previous time of the departure date. She hadn't wanted to think about it and so had refused to think about it.

Now it was almost upon her. She felt so wrecked that she was beyond weeping.

'Well, have you?'

'Have I what?' she managed quite cheekily.

'Dubai. Have you seen pictures of it or any programmes on television?'

'No.'

'What a place! Built by Arab millionaires.'

She might have known that he would admire and be interested in Arabs. He even worked for Arabs in Saudi Arabia, didn't he? Or was it *with* Arabs? What did it matter? Soon he would be back with all these hospitable and friendly Arabs that he admired so much. Friendly and hospitable, he kept calling them. She didn't like the sound of them at all. What kind of men were they that walked hand-in-hand with one another and even kissed each other's cheeks apparently? And women were treated like inferior creatures, by the sound of it, and had to keep covered up from head to toe. She hated the people and the place that was taking Brian away from her.

'I've spent a couple of leaves in Dubai before,' Brian was saying now. 'In my Arab friend's flat. You should see it. It's about the size of a football pitch. You could get lost in it. And his yacht's huge as well.'

She certainly could never compete with all that. A feeling of desolation swept over her as she thought of what it would be like to be without Brian. Frantically she struggled to pull herself together. She had been happy before and she would be happy again. All she had to do was to make the most of their last days together.

They walked back down Sauchiehall Street from the Mitchell and had their evening meal in an Italian restaurant. It was as if he was already halfway back to his home in Saudi Arabia. He kept talking about it. He lived very happily in a lovely little villa in a beautiful compound. He had an excellent houseboy who cleaned the place and cooked all his meals. He was a member of the golf club in the compound and there were evening concerts and dances he attended. Sometimes he'd take a drive out into the desert.

'You wouldn't believe the size of the roundabouts they have there.'

Roundabouts? What on earth was he talking about now?

She felt so broken-hearted she could hardly take in anything he was saying. Especially when he was saying everything so enthusiastically.

At long last, they got back to the Calton and her flat. It suddenly seemed tiny in comparison with what he'd been saying about his Arab friend's magnificent flat in Dubai. But she didn't care about that, she told herself stubbornly, bitterly. She loved her flat in the Barras. There was no place anywhere in the whole world like it. She didn't care what Brian said.

But she did care about him. She didn't know how she'd hide the strength of her caring for him, but she felt she had to try.

He mustn't feel she was being too clingy or making too many unwelcome demands on him. She had been a good tourist guide. At least he had no doubts about that. He'd made that very clear. She also believed he had enjoyed the sex he'd had with her. She wished she could say the word 'lovemaking' but couldn't, not even to herself. After all, the word 'love' had never been mentioned.

That night he undressed her slowly and kissed every part of her from the top of her head to the soles of her feet. The sex they had was passionate.

Sex, sex, never love. But what was the use anyway? Soon he would be gone forever as if he'd never been.

5

He'd gone. Jessica struggled to cope with her grief by immersing herself in the smells and sights and sounds of the Barras.

Nearby there was an Asian vendor who had two stalls separated by an old wooden crate. He was calling out to a lady in a broad Glasgow accent, 'Madam, step into the children's department.'

The air was thick with the smell of doughnuts, hot dogs, candyfloss, fruit stalls and home baking. There was a big queue to buy whelks. Nearby was a stall selling the old Scottish delicacy, the clootie dumpling.

There was also an element of danger or suspense in the air, with touts trying to sell cheap cigarettes and DVDs, and keeping an eye open in readiness to spring away at any sign of a policeman. The police were always in civvies and tried their best to blend in. They never managed to. They were too tall and far too clean.

At the moment, Mrs Mellors was concentrating on woollen goods. She'd made a contact in a sheltered housing complex in Vale of Lennox where she lived. A crowd of lady residents enjoyed a knitting bee in their common room and they knitted everything from scarves and gloves, hats, bedsocks and cot blankets, to beautiful jumpers and cardigans. Mrs Mellors bought them at a giveaway price but one that kept the old residents perfectly happy. She then sold them from her stall at a very much higher price. She had always made a good profit but never such a good one as this. During the week, she supplemented this by making children's kilts, velvet jackets and white frilled shirts. Eventually, she started to knit as well and concentrated on selling woollens.

'Listen Jessie,' she said now. 'You're looking awfu' down in the dumps. Come on, we'll pack up right now and you'll come out wi' me to Vale of Lennox and I'll make you a nice tea. You can stay overnight. In fact, you can stay as long as you like. I'll show you around and introduce you to some nice folk. Most of them work here like me and you, but there's other locals as well. And of course you know my son.'

Jessica hesitated for a moment. It had become quite a torment sleeping alone in her big flat and the Barras area could be a lot quieter during the week.

'OK,' she said eventually, and Mrs Mellors looked delighted.

'Smashing. Come on then, let's get everything packed away.'

In no time at all, Jessica had collected her nightie and a few other things in her overnight bag and was perched beside Mrs Mellors in the van. Normally it would have been Jessica who would chatter all the way. This time she was unusually quiet and it was Mrs Mellors who did most of the talking.

Her cottage was facing the Lennoxtown road across from the Green. Surrounding the Green were a couple of shops, a hotel, a church and a block of flats.

'Look back there, Jessie,' Mrs Mellors said as she opened the door of her cottage. 'See that block of flats. There's a couple vacant in there. You could get one of them no problem. This is a great wee community. Everyone knows one another and we have great social get-togethers. You'd love it here.'

The word 'love' was like a dagger piercing Jessica's heart. She had loved Brian Anderson, still loved him, and believed that she would always love him.

As if reading Jessica's mind, Mrs Mellors said, 'You'll get over him, Jessie. You'll meet other men just as handsome as him, you'll see.'

'Aye, sure,' Jessica said sarcastically.

'Of course you will.' Mrs Mellors' voice became impatient. 'My God, you'd think you were the only one in the world that had fallen for somebody and then got dumped. It happens all the time and I did warn you. But it was so like you not to take a blind bit of notice of what I said. I told you you'd regret it.'

'I don't regret it.'

'What have you got such a long face for then? You're not your usual chirpy, cheeky self at all these days. Even the customers are noticing it.'

Jessica made a supreme effort. She tossed back her curly riot of hair and laughed. 'I've caught one of those bugs that's going about. I'll be fine in a day or two.'

'The flats are nice, aren't they?' Mrs Mellors led Jessica into one of her cheery, chintzy bedrooms. 'Dump your bag on the chair just now and come on through to the kitchen. Help me make the tea. You can unpack later on. You set the table and I'll heat up a nice steak pie I've got in the fridge.'

'I don't really feel like much. A cup of tea and a bit of toast would go down better, I think.'

'Och, try a wee bit of the pie. It'll put some strength into you.'

'OK, OK. Anything you say.'

'What do you think of the flats? We could have a look round one later on tonight if you want. Or tomorrow morning.'

'Mrs Mellors, I've already got a flat. I think it's great. I love it. You know fine I do.'

'But Jessie, you're on your own too much there now, and let's face it – the Calton's a pretty tough area. An innocent, trusting wee lassie like you wandering around on her own there isn't such a good idea.'

'You were born and bred in the Calton and I've never heard you say a word against it before.'

'I know, but it's not the place it used to be and you can be that reckless and stupid at times. I worry about you, Jessie.'

Suddenly Jessica pounced on the older woman, gave her an impulsive hug and showered her with kisses.

'I love you for loving me.'

Mrs Mellors laughed. 'That sounds like a song. Get off me, you daft stick. Set the table like I told you. And believe me, I'm glad of your company now that my family are away in Australia.'

'Oh, I was forgetting about that.' Jessica hugged the older woman even harder. 'I do love you. I'm your adopted daughter, aren't I?'

'Aye, aye.'

After the meal Mrs Mellors insisted that they at least had a walk around the Green, had a closer look at the flats and then enjoyed a drink at the hotel.

In the bar was a crowd of people including a couple of men. Some of them worked in Glasgow. Some of them worked in the Barras. They kept backing Mrs Mellors up in trying to persuade Jessica to make the move to Vale of Lennox.

'This is a great place,' they said. 'It's really beautiful here. Look at the beautiful view of the Campsie Hills.'

Jessica couldn't deny it. The grassy Green, the gardens, the trees and of course the hills rising high up beyond the village were indeed beautiful and peaceful. Too peaceful for her taste, though.

At long last, they returned to the cottage and to bed. Jessica didn't sleep well and awoke in the morning feeling so sick that she barely made it to the bathroom. She was still violently retching when Mrs Mellors came hurrying through.

'Jessie, Jessie.' She put a comforting arm around Jessica's shoulders. 'I'll phone for the doctor.'

'No, no.' The vomiting stopped and thankfully Jessica was able to straighten up.

'Well, get dressed and come through and have a cup of tea and then I'll walk you over to the doctor's surgery. It's just across Abercromby Street.'

'Och, I don't think . . .'

'You'll do as you're told for once,' Mrs Mellors interrupted.

And so they eventually walked arm-in-arm to the doctor's surgery.

'The surgery's in his house,' Mrs Mellors explained. 'He lives there with his mother. She's a right pain in the arse and fancy calling the poor guy Pinkie. Pinkie Plockton, she christened him, and he's been suffering as a result ever since. He's got red hair, which makes it worse. I can just imagine how the poor soul would be tormented at school.'

Dr Plockton had a rather shy but pleasant manner and after he examined Jessica, she and Mrs Mellors sat opposite him at his desk. It was then that he announced that Jessica was pregnant.

'I knew this would happen,' Mrs Mellors cried out. 'I knew that bastard would be too selfish to use a contraceptive.'

'I take it Jessica is your daughter,' Pinkie Plockton said.

'No, no, but I wish she was,' Mrs Mellors said.

'She's like a mother to me,' Jessica managed, but her mind was in a turmoil. She didn't know whether to be pleased or frightened. She felt a bit of both. In one way, she felt glad that something of Brian was inside her and she would have a baby that she could always love as part of him.

In another way she felt frightened at her own ignorance. She hadn't a clue how to look after a baby.

After they had left the doctor's surgery, Mrs Mellors said, 'The least that bastard can do is pay for the kid's upkeep. Take some responsibility.'

Jessica bit her lip worriedly. 'Do you think I should tell him then?'

'Of course you should write and tell him. You've got his address, I hope.'

'Yes, it's this compound place in the desert. He told me where it was and all about it.'

'Well, you'll write to him right away, do you hear? Don't let him get away with it.'

'OK, OK.' She sounded her usual cheeky self, quite sure of herself even. But inside was a different story. She tossed her hair and it bounced about as if she hadn't a care in the world.

Inside she was so near to fainting she didn't dare close her eyes.

6

The clinic in the Calton was there for drop-outs, tramps, prostitutes and any riff-raff who slept in the streets. They needed not only medical treatment but a change of clothes, a wash, a dose of methadone, or even a bowl or soup. They could get it all at the clinic. People donated bags of clothes. If there were decent suits in the bags, the clinic only gave out the trousers. 'The suits are just for a funeral,' they said. And when the suits were given out for funerals, it was just on loan. 'You bring that good suit back,' they were warned, 'or you'll never set foot in here again.'

Jessica had got to know one of the nurses, a young woman called Evie Jeffreys. Evie bought woollens from Mrs Mellors' stall.

'Nobody could get lovely hand-knitted goods like that anywhere else but in the Barras,' she often said. She loved a walk around the market too. Jessica felt a lot in common with Evie as far as the Barras and the Calton in general were concerned. But she couldn't have handled Evie's job at the clinic and greatly admired her kindness and good humour in dealing with some of the worst dregs of humanity. She'd seen Evie giving a sympathetic hug to a down-and-out who stank so much of pee that Jessica, standing yards away, felt unbearably nauseated by it. Now she felt the need to talk to Evie about the problem with her pregnancy. Mrs Mellors kept calling it her 'unwanted pregnancy' and Jessica suspected that Mrs Mellors would be both pleased and relieved if she terminated it in some way. She wasn't sure if she ought to let Brian know anything about it. She didn't want him to think she was mercenary – just out for money.

She phoned Evie and asked if she could come and have a quick word and maybe get a bit of advice.

'Sure,' Evie said. 'I'll find a quiet spot for us.'

The waiting room and some of the corridors were packed with dossers who were drunk, by the sound of their slurred songs. Women too, young and old, drooping with hopelessness.

'Along here.' Evie led Jessica into a small area with shelves all around, filled with files and books.

'What's up?' Evie asked.

Jessica rolled her eyes. 'Remember that guy I told you about? The one from Saudi Arabia that I was crazy about? He's away back and I've just discovered that I'm pregnant.'

'Oh God.'

'I'm still crazy about him but that's neither here nor there because he obviously doesn't feel the same way about me.'

'How do you know that?'

'Well, he never said it to me in so many words. He's away now. Saudi Arabia of all places. Mrs Mellors thinks I should write and tell him and ask for money but I'm not happy with that idea. I don't want him to think I've just been after him for his money.'

Evie thought for a minute. 'Well, I think he deserves to be told that you're expecting his baby, Jessica. That's only fair. I wouldn't say anything about money. Just say you thought it right that he should know you're expecting his child. You could even go further if you like and say that you're looking forward to having the baby and you'll always love and cherish it because you love him.'

31

'Oh.'

'That would be true, wouldn't it?'

'Oh yes.'

'Well then. I think it would be safer and wiser not to show the letter to Mrs Mellors, though. Just tell her you've posted a letter to him and leave it at that. She means well and just wants you to be OK. But I think it might be better just to do as I say this time.'

'Oh Evie, thank you.'

'You're welcome. Now I'd better get back to all the others needing my help and advice. A lot of good it'll do them, though,' she added sarcastically.

'Oh Evie, I'm sure they couldn't do without you. You're marvellous to all of them. I just don't know how you can survive working with people like that.'

'It's their survival that worries me, not mine, Jessica. Now away you go and write that letter.'

Still worried and uncertain in her mind, yet lighter in her heart, Jessica left the clinic. First she had to step over some people lying in the corridor before she could get out. The Calton was a world of its own, she thought, and it looked after its own. In the Calton, folk had always helped one another. Long ago one of its best-known residents, David Dale, was a successful importer of linen yarn which he gave out to all the weavers working at home. One day, he had arranged a dinner for the directors of the Royal Bank. But the Camlachie burn overflowed and flooded his kitchen. The good Calton folk from all around immediately got together to cook the food and save the day.

It was still the same now, Jessica thought. Mrs Mellors was desperately wanting to help her. She meant well but that didn't necessarily mean that she was right. The more Jessica thought about Evie's advice, the more she felt that was what she should do. At least she would be telling the truth and that in itself would be a relief. And it would show Brian that not only had she not been after his money, but she wasn't the type of girl that just slept with anyone who happened to appear at Mrs Mellors' stall. She loved him. That was all that had mattered and was all that mattered still.

As soon as she got back to her flat, she sat down and concentrated on writing an absolutely truthful letter, just as Evie had told her to. It stirred up emotions that she had been keeping in check and she wept over the paper. But she finished it and hurried to post it before her nerve failed her.

'There, it's done,' she thought as it disappeared into the post box. Too late she realised that she should have sent it by airmail. It would have been quicker, but what did speed matter? He would get it eventually.

'I'll have to forget about it now,' she thought. That was the main thing. She was lucky that Mrs Mellors would let her go on working at the stall as usual right up to the birth. And afterwards she could have the pram behind the stall and still work while she looked after the baby.

'I'll always be there to help all I can, Jessie,' Mrs Mellors assured her. She still wanted Jessica to sell the flat above the market, of course, and buy one in Vale of Lennox. All right, Vale of Lennox was a lovely place and she already knew quite a few of the stall holders who lived there, so she would still be among friends. The market and the Calton were her life, however. She couldn't imagine giving them up.

'You'd still be working in the Barras every weekend just the same,' Mrs Mellors insisted.

'I know, I know. But it's my flat and I've still all the memories of my mother and father there.'

Mrs Mellors rolled her eyes. 'You shouldn't cling to the past like that. It's not natural and it's not good for you, Jessie.'

Jessica shrugged. 'I can't help it. Maybe one day, I don't know. But not now.'

Mrs Mellors began knitting baby clothes, not just for the stall but for Jessica as well. She refused to take any payment.

'Would I charge my own daughter?' she asked. 'And I keep telling you you're like a daughter to me. I couldn't ask for a better wee lassie.'

Jessica didn't feel so guilty when – partly due to her hard work and persuasiveness, as well as the good quality of the garments – the stall was doing extremely well. Mrs Mellors was in fact, as she said herself, making a fortune. Most of the stall holders made a very good living. Not everyone was as honest as Mrs Mellors, of course. There were also the men who sold stolen cigarettes and illegal DVDs. They went around shouting 'Cheap fags and DVDs!' if no policemen were around. If there were any police in the area, the men would go around whispering 'Cheap fags and DVDs.'

Jessica tried to put the letter and Brian out of her mind. At least her morning sickness had stopped and she felt physically fit. Sometimes she even felt happy because of the baby. She began to make plans for it, for them both.

Then one day the postman delivered a letter – an airmail letter. Jessica knew right away that it must be from Brian. Who else in the world would be likely to send her an airmail letter?

She stood with it in her hand for a very long time before she gathered enough courage to open it.

7

Jessica danced wildly around the room, around the whole flat. She waved the letter out of the kitchen window and called to the market below.

'He loves me. He loves me. He loves me the same as I love him.'

Not only that. He wanted to marry her.

'We'll get married on my next leave,' he'd written. 'And don't worry. I won't expect you to leave your flat or the Calton. You can stay in your lovely flat as long as you like. I can be there with you every minute of every leave.'

What could be better in the whole world? She couldn't wait to tell Mrs Mellors. She rushed down the stairs to find Mrs Mellors unpacking a box of woollens she'd been busy knitting at home all week.

'Mrs Mellors, Mrs Mellors,' Jessica shouted, jumping up and down.

'Calm down, for pity's sake,' Mrs Mellors said. 'What on earth's happened?'

'I got a letter from Brian and he says he loves me and wants to marry me. He wants us to get married right away on his next leave.'

'Well, thank God he's turned out to be a decent chap after all. I'm very pleased to hear it, Jessie, but sad too.'

'How can you be sad? Isn't this the very best thing that could have happened?'

'For you, yes. For me, it means being without you and that hardly bears thinking about. First my son, and now my daughter.'

'But you won't be without me. Brian knows what my flat and the Barras and you mean to me. He says I can stay here and he'll come over and spend every leave with me.'

Mrs Mellors thought for a minute. 'I suppose that's the best way. I don't know how you'd get on in some god-forsaken place in the middle of the desert. And with the terrible heat I've heard there is out there, it wouldn't be very good for a wee baby. Yes, I think him coming over here is for the best.' She visibly relaxed. 'Congratulations, Jessie. Now, we'll have to start thinking about all the preparations for your wedding.'

'Och, it'll be a month or two yet before he gets over. Before he got my letter, he was due leave and he spent it in Dubai. That's why it'll be another few weeks before he gets another leave. And I seem to be getting fatter by the minute. So it'll have to be a very quiet affair with just you and Evie.'

'I'll knit you a nice loose top. A real pretty one. You'll be fine.'

'Oh thanks, Mrs Mellors.' Jessica pounced on her and gave her an enthusiastic hug. 'You're always so good to me.'

'And you're good to me, Jessie. You work like a slave at my stall.'

'Some slave,' Jessica laughed. 'You know fine I love the work and you pay me well.'

'Not well enough. But I'll knit you a nice top. And maybe one of those capes that drape back across one shoulder.'

'You've already knitted plenty for the baby.'

'Knitting's nothing to me. I can do it with my eyes shut.'

'Oh, but isn't it wonderful, wonderful news that he loves me.'

'Why shouldn't he? He'd be daft if he didn't. You're a very lovable wee lassie.'

'Oh, I don't know about that.'

'Well, I do. Now calm down and help me unpack all this stuff and set it out on the stall.'

Jessica sang as she worked. She had never been so happy in all her life. Now she could have the best of both worlds. Her flat, her Barras, her Calton, and her Brian. Not to mention the baby they had made together that would be part of them both.

What a relief it was that she would not need to go to a strange country and be among strange people in what sounded like a very frightening place. Brian had told her about the terrorist attacks there had been on the compound. He had told her that the terrorists were always successfully repulsed by the armed soldiers who guarded the compound. Nevertheless, it sounded a very scary environment. She would worry about the baby's safety and well-being, as well as her own. It would be bad enough worrying about Brian living there. But he seemed to be well used to the place, he enjoyed his job and had made lots of friends.

Yes, the arrangement he had suggested was best for both of them. She could imagine how it would be like a honeymoon each time he came home on leave. She was indeed the luckiest of mortals.

Mrs Mellors, and then the customers, laughed at her singing so merrily as she worked.

'What's happened to you that's making you so cheery today?' the customers asked.

Flushed with delight, Jessica kept answering, 'I'll be getting married soon.'

'I'm getting married in the morning . . .' Some of the customers burst merrily into the old song. And everyone laughed and it was a lovely happy day. Jessica would never forget it.

And when the day's work was done, Mrs Mellors said, 'Now, you're far too excited. You're not safe to be left on your own in the state you're in. Get in the van and come home with me. You can relax in my peaceful wee cottage until you get back to normal. I'll cook us a nice meal and then we'll enjoy a wee drink in the Abercromby. You can tell your news to all your friends there as well if you like.'

It was the 'tell your news to all your friends there' that tempted Jessica and made her decide to go. She ran upstairs for an overnight bag and was back down, and breathless, within a few minutes.

'You'll have to learn to watch what you're doing, Jessie. You shouldn't be running up and down stairs in your condition.'

'Well,' Jessica laughed, 'I couldn't run very quick and I helped heave myself up and down by grabbing hold of the banisters.'

'Still, look at you, all panting for breath. You'll have to learn to keep calm and slow down.'

'OK. OK.'

'And another thing. When I said you'd be able to tell your friends when you meet them in the Abercromby, I didn't mean you'd to go wild again and jump up and down and shout around as if you've gone off your head.'

'OK. OK. I'll be perfectly calm. Sedate even.'

'That'll be the day.'

Once she was in the van and they'd set off towards the outskirts of the city, Mrs Mellors said, 'Now, we'll talk about all the arrangements for the wedding, and anything else you want to talk about, once we get to my place and have our tea. Meantime, you just close your eyes and relax.'

'OK. OK.'

'That baby of yours will be wondering what on earth is going on with you making it bounce about inside you so much. Seriously, Jessie, you could harm the baby. It could bounce right out if you're not careful.'

'Oh gosh, I never thought of that.'

'Yes, you've not just yourself to think about now. You can't afford to forget that. That wee baby inside you is depending on you to be sensible and not hurt it.'

'I'd never want to hurt it,' Jessica cried out. 'Never, never!'

'Well, just do as I tell you. Close your eyes and calm yourself. And stop trying to run about and jump up and down and get over-excited.'

'Yes, all right.'

Dutifully she closed her eyes and leaned back in the seat. She had been behaving thoughtlessly and foolishly. She realised that now. Would she ever learn? Even now, the mere thought of Brian and seeing him again made her heart flutter and race. She began taking deep, slow breaths.

'That's the way,' Mrs Mellors said. 'Just keep calm and you'll be all right.'

But how to keep calm, to keep calm all the time – that was the problem. If something happened to the baby, she couldn't bear it. It was far too dreadful even to contemplate.

8

'I'm worried now about the baby,' Jessica admitted to Mrs Mellors once they had settled into the Vale of Lennox cottage. 'Really worried.'

'Well, the best thing to do about that and to put your mind at rest is to visit Dr Plockton again for a check-up. We can take a walk over there now and then hopefully we'll be able to relax over a drink in the bar.'

'OK,' Jessica agreed, only too glad of the opportunity of getting checked over to make sure, absolutely sure, she had not done the baby any harm.

Mrs Plockton met them at the door and Mrs Mellors said, 'We haven't an appointment but Jessica here is so upset and worried in case she might have accidentally done something to harm the baby. She's an awful worrier.'

'Come in, come in, my dear girl.' Mrs Plockton put an arm around Jessica's shoulders, drew her away from Mrs Mellors and led the trembling girl into the house. 'I'll look after you now, my dear girl. You'll be all right.' Turning to Mrs Mellors, she added in a cooler tone, 'You wait out there on the garden seat.'

Mrs Mellors flushed with annoyance, but for Jessica's sake she said nothing and went across a well-kept lawn and sat down on the rustic wooden seat. She often felt like saying to

Mrs Plockton, 'You're a two-faced, bullying cow.' In fact, she'd dearly love to give Mrs Plockton a punch in the face.

She had actually once called her a bully of a woman to her face. Thus Mrs Plockton's present hatred of her. Some people of a less strong character had been seduced by Mrs Plockton's gushing sympathetic attention and then found out too late their lives were being taken over and ruled by the woman. Mrs Mellors knew of cases where marriages had been broken up because of Mrs Plockton's insidious hints and lies and accusations against one or other of the marriage partners. Usually they had been perfectly happy together before her interference. Everything Mrs Plockton said or did, of course, was in the guise of heartfelt sympathy.

'You have my heartfelt sympathy, my dear,' she was often heard to say.

She'd once said it to Mrs Mellors and got the immediate retort, 'Go to hell!' She interfered endlessly with Dr Plockton's advice and treatment.

'Dear Pinkie,' she'd say even in front of him. 'The dear boy doesn't understand.'

Mrs Mellors had remarked more than once to her friends, 'Dr Plockton, a good doctor by the way, must often feel like throttling that woman.'

Now, sitting on the garden seat and looking across at the church spire on the Green, she prayed that Jessica would be all right. She could be so easily influenced.

Inside the house, Mrs Plockton was questioning Jessica and encouraging her to talk about not only her worries about the baby but the baby's father and the situation of him travelling from Saudi Arabia to spend his leaves with her and how, after they were married, she would be remaining in her flat in the Calton.

'Oh you poor soul,' Mrs Plockton sympathised. 'He doesn't care about you enough to take you to his place. Doesn't he want to be with you all the time?'

'Oh yes,' Jessica protested. 'He loves me and wants to be with me. He told me in his letter.'

'But not all the time,' Mrs Plockton said gently.

At this point, Mrs Mellors appeared. The door had not been locked and, unable to bear the suspense of what might be happening to Jessica, she'd pushed her way defiantly in.

'You just mind your own bloody business,' she said to Mrs Plockton. 'Now, where's the doctor? That's who we came to see, not you.'

The surgery door opened then, no doubt because Dr Plockton had heard the loud voice of Mrs Mellors.

'Good afternoon, ladies.'

'Good afternoon, doctor,' Mrs Mellors said. 'I've brought Jessica here for a wee check-up. She's worried she might have unintentionally done something to harm the baby.'

'Come through.' He smiled and ushered them into his surgery. Mrs Mellors, always quick on the uptake, caught the quick glance of hatred that he flashed across to his mother.

Ah, I was right, Mrs Mellors thought. The poor guy had suffered so much all his life with that cow of a woman, he would love to throttle her. All the same, she hoped he never would. Not for that old cow's sake, but for his own. It would be too terrible to see such a nice man, and such a good doctor, spend the rest of his life in prison.

After a gentle but thorough examination, Dr Plockton said everything was all right and both babies were fine.

'Both babies?' Jessica and Mrs Mellors cried out in unison.

'Yes. Congratulations, you're expecting twins.'

In a bit of a daze, they thanked him and left his surgery room. Mrs Plockton was waiting to pounce, her face creased with sympathy. Mrs Mellors kept a firm grip of Jessica and forced her to hurry past Mrs Plockton and escape from the house and across the pretty flower-surrounded garden and out to Abercromby Street.

'For God's sake, don't have anything to do with that woman. Never listen to her, Jessie. She's a dangerous troublemaker.'

'She sounded so nice and sympathetic,' Jessica said.

'I bet she did.'

'Right enough, she'd got the wrong idea about Brian.'

'Yes, that's what she does. Puts people against one another. I know more than one couple she's caused to break up and end in the divorce court.'

'Twins!' Jessica echoed in a daze. 'Fancy! Isn't it wonderful! Mrs Plockton wouldn't think anything wrong about that.'

'What? Didn't you believe her so-called sympathy and fall for her talk only a few minutes ago?

'Well, maybe, but I wasn't ever going to believe anything bad about Brian.'

'Good for you. You love him and now you know that he loves you and he's going to marry you. That's all that matters. And I think he's a great guy now that I know he's going to tell you to stay in Scotland where you belong, and with me to keep an eye on you. And he'll be delighted about the twins.'

Jessica laughed. 'Changed days. You didn't always like him.'

'We all make mistakes, Jessie. And I made a mistake about him.'

'The wedding's all settled then. You're giving me away and Evie's to be my bridesmaid but it's going to be a really quiet ceremony. Otherwise it'll be a terrible embarrassment with the size of me.'

'Jessie, has it never occurred to you that by the time Brian gets back, you might have already given birth and you'll be pushing a twin pram to the ceremony?'

'I suppose I could, right enough. But it won't matter, will it? I mean the preacher will still marry me?'

'Of course, you daftie. Why shouldn't he?'

'I must write to Brian right away.'

'Well, for goodness sake, send it airmail this time.'

'OK. OK.'

'And another thing, Jessie. You'd definitely be better and safer staying here with me until after the birth. What if you went into labour on your own in the flat and I was away out here in Vale of Lennox? And you know and like Dr Plockton here and he knows you and your condition. He'd be the best person to deliver your babies.'

Jessica thought for a minute or two. 'I suppose you're right. But are you sure that would be all right with you? It seems an awful imposition.'

'Don't be daft. Aren't you the only family I've got here now?'

Jessica gave her a hug and a kiss. 'Oh, thank you so much. I know how you must miss your own family and I really appreciate all you do for me.'

'I keep having to remind you of all that you do for me. How could I run the stall without you? And by the way, it's time you did as much knitting for it as I do. All right?'

'OK.' Jessica grinned. 'It's a deal.'

Much as she still loved the flat and the Calton, she felt glad to be in Vale of Lennox now and safe in Mrs Mellors' cottage and so near to Dr Plockton. Also, if necessary, it was good to know that the hospital annexe was not too far away at the end of Blair Street. Blair Street ran parallel to Abercromby Street.

The plan nearly went terribly wrong, however. Jessica went into labour just as they were about to leave the stall and drive back to Vale of Lennox.

'Come on, it's just begun,' Mrs Mellors said. 'We'll get back to the cottage in plenty of time.'

'Oh, are you sure?' Jessica was nursing her bulge, her eyes strained with anxiety.

'Yes, come on. Let me help you up into the van.'

With some heaving and difficulty, Mrs Mellors got Jessica on to the van seat and then hurried round to her driving seat. They set off at some speed with both of them busy with silent, fervent prayers.

9

They didn't even have time to get to the hospital. On the way, they called in at the cottage to pick up a case that was all packed and ready with everything Jessica needed for herself and the babies. However, as soon as they reached the cottage, Mrs Mellors had to make an urgent call to Dr Plockton. He was only minutes away, far nearer than the hospital, and he responded immediately to the call. Within minutes, he had delivered a healthy little boy and an equally healthy little girl.

'Nothing wrong with their lungs anyway,' Mrs Mellors laughed. Mrs Mellors washed them and wrapped them and gave them both to Jessica to hold.

Jessica was exhausted but deliriously happy. 'They're OK?'

'Of course,' Mrs Mellors said. 'More than just OK. They're perfect. Right, Doctor?'

Dr Plockton gave one of his shy smiles. 'Yes, indeed. I'll call back to see you tomorrow. Meantime, just rest and relax. Will you manage all right, Mrs Mellors? I could arrange for a nurse.'

'No, no, but thanks all the same, Doctor.'

She saw him to the door and then hurried back to the bedroom, where Jessica was gazing with fervent love and delight at the bundles held in the crook of each arm.

'Well,' said Mrs Mellors, 'this'll be some news for your Brian, eh?'

'Do you think he'll be pleased?' A look of anxiety immediately strained at Jessica's eyes.

'Pleased? He'll be over the moon with pride and delight.'

Jessica relaxed again.

'Fancy me managing to have twins!'

Mrs Mellors laughed. 'Nobody could have done it better. But now we'll have to get you that twin pram. I put the word around as you know, and Bobby from Bobby's Bikes promised you one. I'll send word to him to bring it out here right away.'

'All this is putting you off your knitting for next Saturday's stall.'

'Stop worrying. I've plenty of stuff in reserve and wait till you see. Having a twin pram parked beside the stall will attract loads of extra customers wanting to come closer to admire the babies. And you know me – once I get them to the stall, I'll start the patter and have them buying stuff no bother.'

True to her word, Mrs Mellors' stall had never done such good business and both she and Jessica were nearly run off their feet trying to keep up with the extra sales. Tommy and Fiona were fortunately good babies and just lay gurgling and smiling up at everybody. Though Mrs Mellors said it couldn't be smiling at their age, it was just wind.

'You're awful,' Jessica protested. 'You say it's just wind, but they've beautiful smiles. Everybody says so. Everybody says they're beautiful babies.'

'I know, and you'd better watch they don't grow up spoiled rotten.'

'They are good though, aren't they? They never cry. They don't seem to mind all the noise and crowds. They seem so happy and contented. I'm so glad and happy for them.'

'When's Brian due now?'

'I told you the date ages ago. Now there's only a couple of weeks to go.'

'Oh yes, I booked the meal in that Italian place. You can take the pram in there. Italians are great with children. I don't know any other place that would welcome children like they do.'

'I know. I remember that time we went ages ago and there was a wee girl toddling about and the waiters were making such a fuss of her, patting her head and giving her sweeties and a balloon to hold. I hope Brian'll like my dress.'

'Stop worrying. It's a lovely dress.'

'At least I've got my figure back. He always said I'd a slim, sexy body. I hope he doesn't mind us not having a white wedding. It seemed such a fuss and expense.'

'I told you to stop worrying. If anything, he'll be glad. It would have meant him seeing about a kilt and all the Highland gear. I don't know why men always have to wear the whole kiltie outfit at a wedding.'

'Oh, I like to see a man in a kilt.'

'Well, you'd better keep your eyes and your mind off men in kilts from now on.'

Jessica laughed. 'Brian is, and always will be, enough for me.' She suddenly did a wild dance around, her hand flaying the air. 'I'm so lucky. Oh, so lucky . . .'

'Is that another song or did you just make it up?'

'I wonder if Brian had red hair when he was a baby. That dusting of hair Tommy has is a bit red, isn't it?'

'More like you. You've still a bit of auburn in your hair. I can see it when the sun shines on it. Brian's hair is as black as soot and most likely always has been.'

'Anyway, I stopped Mrs Plockton calling Tommy names. So I'm not as daft as you always make me out.'

'Calling Tommy names?'

'Yes, another wee Pinkie, she said, and when I objected, she patted his head and said, "Yes, maybe wee ginger nut would be better." '

'The cow!'

'I said very firmly, "His name is Tommy and he'll be called nothing else." You would have been proud of me, Mrs Mellors.'

'Good for you, Jessie. But I was just thinking. Are you managing the stairs all right with the pram?'

'You help me get it up and down.'

'When I'm here, but that's just at weekends. I still think you'd be much better in Vale of Lennox during the week. And I'm sure Brian will think the same. He likes the Campsie area, doesn't he?'

'Yes, he used to do a lot of hillwalking and climbing when he was young, he told me.'

'There you are then.'

'I'm fine just now. I'm managing the pram up and down the stairs.' Her feelings about the flat and it being such an intimate part of the market hadn't changed. She still loved it.

However, Brian agreed with Mrs Mellors after he came home and saw the struggle she must be having with the pram.

'But I'm going to get one of those smaller buggies when the twins are a bit older, and better at sitting up.'

'Yes, older and heavier, Jessica.'

'But I can't leave my flat. You know that.'

'Just during the week. You can still be in your flat every weekend when Mrs Mellors would be there to help you with the pram.'

'I bet she's been on at you about the flats in Vale of Lennox.'

'Yes. However, she also said you could stay with her in the cottage if you still don't want to take on one of the flats there.'

Jessica tutted and shook her head.

'I wish the pair of you would stop nagging at me.'

Brian enfolded her in his arms and kissed her brow, her cheeks, her lips.

'Darling, I'm only thinking of what's best for you. And I'm sure Mrs Mellors is too.'

'OK. OK. I'll think about it. I'll just think about it. I'm not going to be rushed into anything.'

But she was still in the Calton flat when Brian came on his next leave. The children could toddle about by then. She could even take their hands and help them to climb the stairs, one on either side of her. Once in the flat, she'd stand them in their high-sided cots and then race back down for the buggy that had replaced the bigger pram. Several more leaves later, the twins were ready to go to the local primary school.

'Talk about being spoiled at the Barras!' Mrs Mellors said. 'Now their daddy spoils them as well. If he brings them any more presents, you won't have enough room in the flat for them all.'

Jessica laughed. 'But they're so adorable, aren't they?'

'Yes, I know, but it's not good for them, Jessie. It might get them into trouble at school. Other kids might resent them and try to bully them. Even the teachers might not like spoiled kids.'

'Now you're worrying me.'

'Just warning you.'

Jessica knew in her heart the truth of what Mrs Mellors was saying. What to do about it, that was the problem. By the time Tommy and Fiona were seven, Jessica could see that they were indeed being picked on. They were suffering fear and unhappiness. On more than one occasion, they had come home clinging to one another and weeping broken-heartedly. In much distress, Jessica had gone to the school to speak to the head teacher in an effort to find out exactly what was going on.

The head teacher had been polite but cool. She would look into the matter, of course, but she was sure, she said, that no bullying or wrongdoing could take place within the confines of her school. The staff supervised behaviour in the playground and would never allow any bullying to take place.

Jessica felt this was not exactly true. There had been times when she'd gone to the school gates at play time with a cake or a bag of sweets for the twins and she had not seen any sign of any teachers.

Something had to be done. She couldn't go on watching the children be scared of going to school and seeing their obvious distress and unhappiness.

She eventually spoke to Brian about it on his next leave.

'There doesn't seem to be anything I can do,' she told him.

'Darling,' he said quickly, 'of course there's something.'

'What?'

'You can bring them out to Saudi and stay with me and be together all the time as a proper family. There's a nursery school and a primary school. There would be a lot fewer children, compared with the big school they attend here. The children all love it in the compound. I'm sure Tommy and Fiona will love it too.'

Jessica was speechless. She had never considered uprooting herself and leaving everything she'd been used to all her life and going to live in a strange, far-off land.

Now, for the first time, she began to consider it.

10

She couldn't do it. Yes, something had to be done. Each day, she'd take the children to school and then wander around the Calton area treasuring every sight and sound and smell. The streets were so lovingly familiar to her. She'd toddled around them when she was little more than a baby. She remembered being fascinated by the escapologist setting up shop on the road, being locked into thick chains, and then getting out of them. She remembered Saturdays and Sundays when crowds streamed into the Barras. She remembered the smells. There were hot roasted chestnuts and salty-smelling whelks. You could get a little pin with the whelks to pull them out of their grey shells. There was the tangy smell of old cheeses – big slices of strong Scottish cheddar and racks of mature yellow and cream-coloured cheeses, some the size of small barrows. The smell of poultry too – rows of birds hanging up, plucked and ready. The fusty smell of potatoes from shopping bags. Pungent sweat squeezing from innumerable armpits. The shouts of stall holders and shopkeepers. The babble of passers-by, the laughter.

Jessica crushed through the crowded streets, her mind overflowing with memories. Soon she found herself outside the drop-in centre and decided to visit Evie. As usual, she had to climb over drunken bodies slumped in passageways. Sad songs slurred from loose mouths. As usual, she marvelled at Evie being able to spend so much time in the place. On this occasion, she was lucky in the fact that Evie was able to go out for lunch.

'We've got enough staff now to take over for an hour and help at lunch time, so each of us can get out if we want to.'

'I'm glad to hear it,' Jessica told her. 'You need to get right away for a decent break. Come on, I'll treat you to lunch at the St Enoch Centre.'

They chatted about Evie's work on the way to the St Enoch Centre and when they reached it, Jessica said, 'Did you know that this is the largest glass-roofed structure in Europe?'

Evie laughed. 'Still the Glasgow historian? I agree with what Brian said, Jessica. You would have made a marvellous tourist guide.'

'He wants more from me than that now.'

'How do you mean?'

'He wants me to go out to Saudi and that awful compound place and live with him and the children there.'

'The compound might not be as bad as you imagine. And he's not wanting something *from* you. He wants to be fully committed to you, share his life with you and the children all the time. Not just for a few weeks a year. Why did you say he's wanting something *from* you?'

Jessica shrugged. 'My life here and all my memories, I suppose.'

'Well, I know how much you're attached to the Calton. I can understand that. You've been here since you were born. All the same, Jessica, he's your husband. Your place is now with him.'

Jessica gave a big sigh.

'I know you're right, of course. It's just . . . It's such a big decision to make – not just moving to another town or even to another country, but to such a strange place, and from what I can gather, a dangerous one too.'

'Oh, I'm sure Brian wouldn't put you or the children in any danger. Every time I've met him, Jessica, he couldn't take his eyes off you. He obviously adores you and the twins.'

Jessica smiled weakly. 'I know. I'm just being stupid.'

'No, you're not. As I said, I can understand how you feel. Apart from being brought up here, it's a very different and quite fascinating place. Not so much nowadays, though. You must admit, Jessica, there isn't the same hilarious patter, for instance, as there used to be.'

'No, but it's still fascinating and full of life and noise and bustle. I like that. I seem to thrive on it, in fact.'

'I thought you loved Brian and found him fascinating.'

'Oh, I do. I do.'

'Well, you won't want to lose him then, will you?'

'Oh no.'

'Decision time then, Jessica.'

'I know. It's just not easy, that's all.'

'It might be a good idea to take the children and go and stay with Mrs Mellors for a week or two and break yourself away from here in a more gradual way.'

'I might just do that. Mrs Mellors is so good about everything. She's going to help me with the sale of the flat, if that's what has to be done eventually. Oh, it's such a thought for me – such a final step to take – to sell that lovely, lovely flat.'

'Oh stop it, Jessica. Brian's got a gorgeous house for you in Saudi Arabia. I've seen the photos of his villa there, remember.'

'I'm sorry. I'll keep my mouth shut about the flat, the Barras and the Calton in future, I promise.'

'All right. I'll keep you to that. Now, it's time I was making my way back to work and you've got the children to collect from school. Get a bag packed and get out to Vale of Lennox right away, do you hear?'

Jessica nodded and arm-in-arm they left the St Enoch Centre and made their way back to the Calton.

Once back in the flat with the children, Jessica did as Evie had told her. She also phoned Mrs Mellors, of course, just to confirm that her visit would be all right. Mrs Mellors was delighted and insisted on driving in to the Calton to collect her and the twins.

'You stay in Vale of Lennox with me for as long as you like,' Mrs Mellors told Jessica. Laughing, she added, 'Stay forever if you want. That's how welcome you and the wee ones are, and always will be.'

It was Jessica's turn to laugh.

'Don't you complicate my life any further. Brian wants me and the twins to go over to Saudi and live with him there until he retires from that job of his in the compound. It's difficult enough for me to think of leaving the Calton. You know only too well what it means to me.'

'Yes, love, but your place is with your good man. I've told you that already.'

'I know. It's just not so easy to uproot myself.'

'I found that out, didn't I, when I tried to get you to come here even for one night, at first. You wouldn't budge from that precious flat of yours. Now you're quite happy to come here and you'll be happy in Brian's place in Saudi Arabia once you get there, I bet.'

'I'm sure you're right.'

'And another thing, Jessie. It's selfish of you to hang on to that flat when so many big families working in the Barras need a decent-sized place. Or any place to stay in the area.'

'OK. OK. Let's give the subject a rest for the moment. Where are the twins?'

'Out in the garden. It'll do them good. They've been looking so pale and strained lately.'

'Yes, I can't go on as we are when I know they're being bullied at school. They're definitely not happy.'

'There you are then.'

Yes, there she was, having to leave the flat, the Calton, Glasgow and Scotland, and travel far away to a strange land.

II

As they passed through King Khalid Airport in Riyadh, Jessica was astonished. There was a call to prayer and the Saudis converged on a huge carpet in the airport concourse where they all stood in a line, as though they were in a mosque, in full view of all the other passengers. All the non-Muslim travellers just continued going about their business.

Brian smiled and nudged her. 'That's a sure sign you're in the Kingdom of Saudi Arabia. By the way, the Kingdom is sometimes called "The Land of the Two Holy Mosques" – that's referring to Mecca and Medina, the two holiest places in Islam. It's just in English it's most commonly referred to as Saudi Arabia.'

The children were trotting along in silence between them, obviously overawed by the strangeness of the place.

'Did you know,' Brian went on enthusiastically, 'that Saudi Arabia is the world's largest petroleum exporter? Oil accounts for more than ninety per cent of exports and nearly seventy-five per cent of government revenues, which has made them able to create a welfare state.'

'A welfare state?' Jessica echoed incredulously.

'Oh yes, it's a marvellous place to live, darling. You'll love it once you get to know it. You and the children will be happy here. I wouldn't have asked you to come if I hadn't been sure of that.'

Suddenly Tommy spoke up. 'The men are wearing dresses.'

Brian laughed. 'It's called a dishdasha or a thoub. It's nice and loose and allows the air to circulate and cool their bodies in the hot summer days. It's white too because white reflects sunlight. That scarf-like thing covering their heads is called a shumagg. There's another thing they wear underneath it to hold their hair in place and the black band around the top of the head holds all the head gear in place. The head cover is always white in summer and heavy red and white checked in winter.'

Fiona asked, 'Do ladies wear the same?'

'No, they wear black coverings called abayas.'

'Oh right.' Jessica raised a sarcastic eyebrow. 'So it doesn't matter about them being cool and having sunlight deflected.'

'It's just the custom in public.' Brian's voice acquired a slight edge. 'It's to do with modesty. But they can wear smart clothes underneath and at home in private. Look at some of them over there with their designer handbags and gold bracelets. They're all right, believe me.'

He used to laugh at her, Jessica thought, and say she wouldn't hear a word against Scotland, especially Glasgow and the Calton. Now it was obvious that he didn't like one hint of criticism of Saudi Arabia and any of its customs.

'And by the way,' Brian went on, 'women have a great deal under Islam compared with what they had before. Nobody wanted a daughter because for one thing she could be an economic burden, so they used to kill them. In some places, they buried them alive.'

'Oh!' Fiona squealed in distress, and Jessica protested angrily, 'Brian, for pity's sake!'

'Sorry, sorry.' He bent down and kissed Fiona. 'I shouldn't have mentioned that, darling. I'm sorry. It was long, long ago and would never, never happen now. I just mentioned it to show what a marvellous difference and happy change the Muslim religion and the Arab rule have made to this country.'

They found their connecting flight and eventually arrived in Tabuk Airport. It was quite small – probably something like the size of Inverness Airport, Jessica guessed.

It was decided that they should have a look around the town of Tabuk before making their way by car to the compound. Brian had left his car in the airport car park.

This was where, Brian told her, she would have to do most of her shopping. She soon realised the reason why Brian sometimes felt compelled to visit somewhere else to pick up some non-Arab food. In fact, most non-Arab people brought enough supplies from their own country to last until their next holiday.

'I've never felt the need to go that far,' Brian said. 'Actually, I enjoy most of the Arab food. It's not that there's anything wrong with any of it. It's just I sometimes miss daft things like Marmite.'

So it was his fault – not anything remotely wrong with anything Arab. Of course, maybe he was right, Jessica thought. Maybe she would grow to love the place and be as happy there as he was. It must have something wonderful about it to engender such love and loyalty as Brian obviously had for it.

She determined to give it a go and try her best to settle down in the compound and be content with life there. She must try not to be sarcastic and critical. After all, she tried to tell herself, not everything about Scotland was perfect. There was a growing crime problem, especially with knives. She had no personal knowledge of this but she had read about it in the papers. There was a drink problem and not only around Evie's drop-in centre. Lots of young people with good jobs and from good homes were apparently binge drinking (again she'd only read about it in the papers). She'd seen pictures of young girls lying helpless on pavements in the city centre. Innumerable drunken young men and women were spilling out of nightclubs at three in the morning.

It wasn't the Glasgow she knew personally but it must be true when it was reported so often in the newspapers and on television.

She didn't want to remember or to think of those things at all, but she was struggling now to be fair and to understand how Brian felt. And as he had said, he wouldn't have brought them over if he hadn't been sure she and the children would love the place and be happy there.

And her love for him hadn't changed. She only had to look at his deeply tanned face and dark eyes to feel a thrill of love for him. Tenderness too. There was something lovable about his loyalty to the country in which he now lived and worked. Loyalty was a good characteristic and she had to admire him for it.

They decided to pick up Brian's car and drive to Aqaba for some rest and recuperation. 'It's on the Red Sea,' Brian said, 'and has great hotels and restaurants.' Smiling, he added, 'And you can get alcohol. No alcohol is allowed in the compound and most other places, but who needs it?'

It turned out that Aqaba was a three-hour drive from Tabuk and the children fell sound asleep in the back of the car. But Brian assured Jessica that the journey would be well worth it. Aqaba was a place of great historical significance. 'You can view three continents and four countries from one place. Aqaba is the geographical focal point of where Egypt, Israel, Jordan and Saudi Arabia all converge.'

Jessica wondered if she had sounded like this when she had been showing Brian around Glasgow. She couldn't resist saying, 'Are you trying to outdo me by being a first-class tourist guide?'

He laughed. 'You were wonderful, darling.'

Once they had booked into a luxurious hotel and were enjoying a good meal, she felt more relaxed. Then, after they had put the children to bed and got into bed themselves, Brian made love to her. It was then all her physical passion for him was reawakened. He brought her to vibrant life. He was her life. She couldn't live without him and wouldn't live without him. Where he went, she would always go. Where he stayed, she would stay.

She even began to look forward to her new life in the compound in Saudi Arabia.

12

The compound was to some degree as Brian had previously described it. Yet she had not been prepared for the shock of the high walls topped with barbed wire. Heavily armed Saudi guards surrounded the walls to protect against terrorist attacks. The dry baking heat caused the walls to appear to shimmer and wobble as if seen from under water. The searing heat seemed to dry up the insides of Jessica's nose as she breathed in.

Jessica was, however, pleasantly surprised by the inside of the compound. The accommodation, she discovered, and the landscaping were maintained to a very high standard. As far as the eye could see, there were pretty flower-lined streets and attractive buildings. Servants continually sprayed water to prevent the plants shrivelling up in the glaring sunshine. She soon forgot about the intimidating walls and guards. She was now in what looked like a small country town with well-kept gardens and pretty villas. Some were three-bedroomed houses for families and that's what Brian had now been allocated. There was also bachelor accommodation and shared bachelor accommodation. Out on verandas, people sat happily chatting and drinking tea or coffee – no alcohol was allowed.

'There's the primary school,' Brian told her as he showed her around.

Inside one of several teachers working there welcomed them and the children.

'We take children from four to eleven years,' she said, 'and we aim at not only the three Rs, but emotional well-being and physical health. I'll show you the exercise room we have. The children love it. We try to make everything fun.'

Certainly Tommy and Fiona took to the place immediately and began running around all the brightly coloured furniture and inspecting all the games laid out on tables and the computers and other teaching equipment.

Jessica laughed. 'They obviously love it already.'

'You can leave them here just now if you like while your husband shows you the rest of the compound.'

'OK. I'll see what they say first.'

She went over to talk to the twins, who were delighted to stay for a while until she and Brian returned to collect them.

Jessica remarked to Brian as soon as they returned outside, 'It's great that the school and our house are air-conditioned. Are all the buildings like that?'

'Oh yes. Otherwise, in this heat, nobody would be fit for anything. I often wonder how the locals manage to survive without it.'

Near the school there was the Sunbeam Centre for younger children. Then around the corner and down another street was Brian's office. He was one of the managers responsible for the running of the compound. He was also an adviser to men who came on business to Saudi.

A swimming pool in another street sparkled in the day-long sunshine.

'There's the golf course and the club house.' They stopped in the club house and enjoyed a long drink of lemonade with plenty of ice chinking in it.

Jessica very quickly came to the conclusion that life in the compound could indeed be absolutely wonderful. Of course, there were restrictions, especially for women. They were never introduced to Arab men, for instance, to Brian's Arab friends. Outside of the compound, woman had to wear the abaya, the national dress for women. Jessica thought it must be similar to what she'd heard of as the burka. One of the Eastern stall holders in the Barras had spoken of woman in his home country having to be all covered up in what he called the burka.

'Gosh, look at it,' Jessica complained to Brian after she bought one. 'It's so depressing having to be all in black like this. It's bad enough to be covered up.'

'Well, you'd better wear it, darling, unless you want to be arrested and even whipped. Once in Saudi we're beyond the protection of our own government. We're totally subject to Saudi Islamic law.'

Another thing Jessica railed against was the fact that women weren't allowed to go anywhere outside the compound on their own. They always had to be accompanied by a man.

'Oh, and another thing,' Brian said, 'when we go visiting one of my Arab friends, you'll be kept separate in another room. But don't worry, you'll still be made welcome by the women.'

Jessica rolled her eyes. 'Talk about discrimination!'

'Oh, there's lots of restrictions on men as well.'

'How do you mean?'

'Well, I've got to remove my shoes before entering any place I'm visiting. And, most important, I've always to remember to eat with my right hand. Even if I was left-handed, I'd still have to use only my right hand. The left hand is considered unclean. You mustn't even gesticulate with your left hand. Oh, and you must never show an Arab the soles of your feet. That's considered offensive.'

'Sounds a whole lot of daft nonsense to me.'

'It's their customs and while we're living in their country, I think it's only fair to try to respect their ways.'

'OK. OK. Fair enough, but I just wish they'd respect our ways in our country.'

'I don't know if you've noticed but a traditional Saudi greeting between men is each grasping the other's right hand, placing the left hand on the other's right shoulder and exchanging kisses on each other's cheek. Everything's done closer together here, even just talking, and it can be insulting to draw back.'

'I've noticed all right. Fancy if they acted like that in the Calton. Can you imagine? The mind boggles!'

Brian laughed. 'What worries me is having to keep someone from the Calton like you in the background. I don't know how I'm going to keep you under control.'

Jessica gave him a mock punch. 'Don't even try.'

But of course they were both forced to obey the rules. Even inside the compound, despite the heat of the desert, Brian had to wear clothes that covered his body – no shorts or short-sleeved shirts were ever allowed. Jessica had to wear high necklines and sleeves reaching at least to the elbow. Hem lines had preferably to be ankle length. Soon strolling around the compound and lazing about on the veranda all day became boring. The children were at school or being supervised by the teachers in after-school recreational activities and so were away from the villa the whole day. It wouldn't have been so bad if she could have busied herself with cooking and housework, but the Indian houseboy always rushed to do everything. He considered it an insult if she tried to do anything around the house.

Thankfully, she managed to find a part-time job helping in one of the cafés. The café offered everything from coffee and cakes to a cooked meal. She only helped clear the tables and fill the dish-washing machine and so she had plenty of opportunity to have a chat and laugh with the others who worked in the café and with the customers as well. They all exchanged stories about where they'd come from and what they'd done before arriving in Saudi. They all agreed it was a wonderful life. Except for the terrorist raids, of course, but they had always happened at night and were quickly fought off by the Saudi guards. The raids were so infrequent that they didn't really impinge on daily routine.

'You'll soon get used to the raids,' they told her. It was hard to believe at first but it had worked out exactly as they'd said.

She and Brian would be sitting watching television, or later, reading in bed when the siren would go. They would get up, lift the soundly sleeping Tommy and Fiona and go with them into the panic room, where there were beds to lie on. Eventually, they'd hear two blasts of the siren which meant everything was safely over and the steel wall of the panic room would be raised. It was an inconvenience more than anything else, and it didn't happen all that often.

No, the worst inconvenience was not being able to share the generous hospitality that Brian always received from his Arab friends. That is, to share it with him. Today he had been invited to the house of Faiz.

'I'm treated like a king,' Brian told her when they neared the house of Faiz. 'Nobody in the world is as kind and hospitable as the Arabs. That room at the front of the house is a typical meeting room and has cushions all around the floor to sit on. These meeting rooms are called majalis. I never meet any of the female members of the family – only brothers and uncles and male cousins. Guests come and go all the time in the majalis.'

'Where will I go then?' Jessica asked.

'You go round the back. Don't worry, one of the women will be waiting for you and will take you in to meet all the other women in the family. They'll probably treat you like a queen. But for God's sake, watch what you say. Saving face, avoidance of shame and keeping dignity are vital to Saudis.'

'Why on earth would I want to shame them?'

'You wouldn't mean to, Jessica. You'd just think you were kidding. But they don't understand that. So just try and keep your mouth shut. That'll be the safest way.'

'For God's sake,' Jessica gasped impatiently. 'What a carry on!'

'You'll get used to it. Just relax and enjoy the tasty titbits they'll feed you with.'

'As if I'm a rabbit or something? What about my dignity?'

'Darling, we can have a fight once we're back home, but please, not here.'

They didn't fight, though. On the way home, she was so taken up with the novelty of her experiences that she forgot about the fight. The camels strolling across the road for instance, with slow dignity, their large feet causing small puffs of dust as they slapped down. Then there were the roundabouts in the desert.

'Look at that one,' Brian said. 'The Arabs like to do everything in a big way. Have you ever seen anything like that in your life?'

Around the city of Tabuk were these roundabouts with gigantic structures in the centre. The one Brian was pointing at had a huge aircraft balanced high on top of it. Then there was one with a tank perched on it.

'All very military-looking, though,' Jessica said.

Brian shrugged. 'It's got an interesting history. There's an ancient mosque where the prophet Mohammed prayed for twenty days.'

Back in the compound they collected Tommy and Fiona from the supervised playpark where most of the children, including Tommy and Fiona, were enjoying riding about on scooters and bikes. They all went for a swim to cool off and afterwards had a meal in one of the dining halls. Then they went to the post office to see if there was any mail for them to collect. They also had a look at the noticeboards for details about all the clubs, events and company notices.

There was no mail for Jessica but an official-looking letter for Brian.

'Good God!'

'What's up? Not bad news, I hope,' Jessica said.

'On the contrary. A distant relation of my father's has left me a house and quite a bit of land on the Campsie Hills.'

'Gosh! Will that be near Vale of Lennox? I know a lot of folk there – including Mrs Mellors, of course.'

'No, it must be a good bit further up than that. I've never seen it even with all the walking I've done in the area.'

'Gosh! What are you going to do about it?'

Brian shrugged. 'I suppose we'd better go and have a look at it on my next leave.'

'You could sell it and get a lot of money for it if it's a big place with a lot of land.'

Brian laughed. 'Trust you to think like that.'

'Well, what else is there?'

'I'll have to retire eventually. It might be a good place to retire to.'

'But that's years yet, isn't it?'

'Yes, but according to this letter, there's a housekeeper and a handyman living in the house. They could continue living there and looking after the place until I retire.'

'You could maybe even rent it out for a few years.'

'Darling, it's not a question of money. I've an enormous salary here. I don't need any extra money.'

'Gosh, there can't be many folk like you going around. You're the only one I've ever met, anyway.'

'Well, I've been earning this salary for quite a few years and there's so many perks and freebies. Also there's very little you can spend money on here. So money piles up in the bank.'

'Nice work if you can get it.'

'And I've got it.'

'So we'll at least go and look at this place in the Campsies?'

'Definitely. On my next leave.'

Jessica did one of her excited little dances and clapped her hands.

'I'll really look forward to that. It'll be a great adventure.'

Brian's voice took on a tone of mock drama. 'A journey into the unknown.'

13

They left the children with Mrs Mellors in Vale of Lennox and started driving towards Hilltop House, at the other side of the Campsies. Eventually, however, they were forced to abandon the car and started walking, or climbing to be more accurate. It wasn't that the terrain was too steep for the car. The place was so overgrown with huge rhododendrons and laurels fighting for space with broom and bracken, such a dark jungle, that it blocked out the sun. They had to fight their way through climbing plants that had grown completely out of control, like the ivy underfoot that they kept sinking into or tripping over. Other spiky high climbing plants crushed together, creating a sinister atmosphere. There were huge trees blocking their path too. The soft gurgling sound warned of a small waterfall almost hidden by plants and shrubs.

'The first thing we'll have to do here,' Brian said, 'is get a landscape gardener to clear the place and make something decent of it.'

'I can't imagine what on earth could be done to make all this look decent.'

'That's their job. They have the imagination. They do this sort of thing all the time – transform estates.'

'OK. OK. I'll believe you.'

Suddenly Brian cried out, 'There it is. God, what a place!'

A large black edifice reared up above the trees.

Jessica shuddered. 'Real creepy!'

'Stop worrying. We could make it really beautiful and impressive. If we got the house painted and the land cleared, it would be a place to be proud of.'

'And feel happy and at home in?' Jessica asked sarcastically.

'Yes. We're very lucky to have received such a legacy. And Jessica, if it suits you better, think of it as a huge money bonus. This place could be worth a fortune, especially with so much land. But wait a minute. I've just had another idea. We could eventually make it into a hotel. That would be a great investment, a continuous income for us.'

Jessica's voice acquired a more interested and cheerful tone.

'Right enough. All sorts of people would come from all over, I bet. I'd enjoy all the company.'

'Yes, think of it as an investment.'

At least there was a little clearing around the house and they climbed the couple of steps at the front and rang the bell. It clanged and echoed loudly through the jungle hush.

A tall, large-busted woman answered.

'You must be Mr and Mrs Anderson, the new owners,' she greeted them. 'Welcome to Hilltop House. I'm Mrs Peterson, the housekeeper.'

They followed her inside. There they stopped to stare in astonishment at walls festooned with antlers and dead animals' heads and skins. Even a tiger skin stretched across one area. The wood panelling was almost black with age.

Mrs Peterson explained, 'The late Mr Nairn used to travel abroad on shooting expeditions and had lots of shooting parties here too. He wasn't fit enough to enjoy them towards the end. The last one was with pheasants that he reared and the guests stayed here for a few days during their shoot. Will you be doing the same, Mr Anderson?'

Jessica answered before Brian could draw his breath.

'No way! Fancy enjoying killing poor animals. I've never heard the like of it in my life. No way!'

'Mr Anderson?' Mrs Peterson repeated in a cooler tone.

Brian treated her to one of his most charming smiles.

'Please forgive my wife, Mrs Peterson. She's always had a soft-hearted and impulsive nature. But no, I don't think we're likely to go in for the shooting business. I have a different career.'

'I see. Follow me and I'll show you around the house. We'll start from the lower floor.'

They all descended a staircase and came to a lower level. A long corridor had several doors leading off from it. Mrs Peterson opened the nearest one to reveal a large stone-flagged kitchen. A man was sitting at a wooden table in the centre of the room. He rose and Mrs Peterson said, 'This is my husband, Geordie. He acts as a handyman doing odd jobs around the house. It's a big place and it entails a great deal of work.'

'It must do,' Brian agreed, 'and would you and Mr Peterson . . .'

'Geordie,' the man interrupted as they shook hands.

'Geordie,' Brian corrected himself, 'agree to go on living and working at Hilltop House even though my wife and I would not be able to settle here for some considerable time?'

'Certainly,' Mrs Peterson said. 'This is obviously the kitchen. The other doors along the corridor lead into the staff living quarters. Upstairs . . .' She led them out again, 'is the main hall that you've seen and along here is the dining room.'

She opened a door to the left of the hall stairway to reveal a large room with a long table and a sideboard groaning under the weight of many bottles of wine and spirits.

'On the next floor is the sitting room, or drawing room.'

They followed the tall stiff-backed woman up the staircase with the ornate carved banisters to another equally shadowy landing.

The room was huge and furnished with floral padded suites and antique-looking chairs that Jessica said afterwards she had been far too nervous to sit on. The windows looked out on to the jungle.

Brian said, 'By the way, we have friends in Vale of Lennox and so we're staying there this time. I've got a couple of months' leave and I think the first thing I must do while I'm here is to try and find a good landscape gardener. Do you happen to know of one?'

Mrs Peterson shook her head. 'No.'

'Don't worry. I'll advertise and hopefully be able to find someone before I'm due back in Saudi. And there'll be plenty of room for whoever I find to live in, won't there?'

'There's ample accommodation for a large staff but Mr Nairn never needed anyone except me and a couple of women from the village when there was a live-in shooting party.'

Already she was leading them up another flight of stairs. 'This is where all the main bedrooms are.' She opened the first door to reveal a wood-panelled room and a huge four-poster bed.

'The other bedrooms are all similar to this one. Do you wish to inspect them all?'

'No, no,' Jessica managed. 'We get the picture.'

'That smaller staircase over there,' Mrs Peterson said, 'leads to rooms for the children and toilet facilities.'

'Were there ever children living here?' Jessica asked incredulously.

'I have only worked for Mr Nairn here, no one else. Until now,' she added without warmth or enthusiasm. But as they descended the stairs again, she did say in a more kindly tone,

'You'll be needing a cup of tea now. I'll put the kettle on and I have some home-baked scones I think you will enjoy.'

'Well, that's most kind of you, Mrs Peterson, but we did promise Mrs Mellors, a friend in Vale of Lennox, that we'd be back to her in time for tea.'

'Very well.'

'Perhaps next time,' Jessica said, 'and I'll look forward to sampling your home baking.'

'Very well,' Mrs Peterson repeated but in a more relaxed and pleasant tone. 'I'll see you to the door. Would you like Geordie to accompany you and direct you?'

Brian said, 'Thank you but we should manage all right. The path's very overgrown but it's still a recognisable path.'

They waved Mrs Peterson goodbye and set off back down the long trek to where they had left their car. After they were safely out of earshot, Jessica said, 'Do you still think it's possible for us to make a hotel of it one day?'

'Remember what I said. It could be an excellent investment. Try to imagine it after a good landscape gardener had cleared it all and made a lovely colourful place of it. And in time, we'll get a house painter to do the same for the house. It could be a beautiful showplace. Stripped wood, new windows, a conservatory out from the lounge.'

'I don't know if I've got that much imagination.'

'You just wait and see. First of all, I'll have to put adverts all around for a landscape gardener.'

'You'll be lucky if you find anyone who'd be able or who'd even want to tackle a job like that.'

'We can but try, darling. For goodness sake, cheer up. I thought you liked challenges. You were always good at taking them on in the Calton. Mrs Mellors told me you could sell a refrigerator to an Eskimo.'

Jessica laughed.

'OK. OK. Everything in the garden – and the house – is going to be lovely. Lovely . . . Lovely . . .' She burst into song as they stumbled and groped their way through the dense jungle.

14

'I told you,' Jessica said after waiting a week for a phone call in answer to the advert they'd put in several newspapers. 'Any gardener who knows what a jungle the place is will give it a wide berth.'

Then Brian got a phone call from an Irishman who said he might be interested.

Jessica laughed then. 'It needed some daft Irishman who's never seen the place to reply. But wait until he does see that jungle. That'll be that.'

Brian arranged for the man – Patrick O'Rourke – to come to Mrs Mellors' cottage and from there they'd repeat the journey Jessica and Brian had already made to Hilltop House.

Patrick O'Rourke turned out to be a handsome man. He didn't have Brian's black hair and tanned skin. He was good-looking in a different way with his slim body and his straight blond hair tied back and blue eyes that crinkled up when he smiled. He was certainly full of Irish charm and blarney.

'It'll have to be a devil of a jungle to defeat Patrick O'Rourke,' he told them.

'Just wait until you see it,' Jessica said.

'Jessica, will you hold your tongue for once.' Brian sounded tense and annoyed.

'OK. OK.'

Once out of the car, they began struggling along the overgrown path.

'Well, Mr O'Rourke,' Jessica said. 'What do you think?'

'Patrick, please.'

'OK, Patrick, what do you think now?'

'I love a challenge. I'll enjoy taming this place.'

Brian said, 'You'd have to live in Hilltop House, Patrick.'

'Yes, that suits me. I was needing a place to lay my head.'

When they reached the house, it only took O'Rourke a few seconds to charm Mrs Peterson and melt her stiff manner.

'What a wonderful woman you obviously are, Mrs Peterson, to be able to live in such isolation and continue to be such a loyal and conscientious worker.'

Jessica could hardly contain a groan at such flattery and was only prevented from saying something by a warning glare from Brian.

The upshot of it all was that Mrs Peterson promised to have the best downstairs room ready for Patrick as soon as he arrived back to start work.

'And, although I say it myself, Patrick, I'm an excellent cook. I think I can safely say that you'll enjoy your food.'

O'Rourke gave a huge sigh of pleasure.

'Ah, what a lucky fellow I am.'

'So you'll definitely accept the job?' Brian asked.

'Definitely, Mr Anderson.'

'Brian.'

'Brian and . . .?' He smiled over at Jessica and she returned his smile.

'Jessica.'

'Jessica,' he repeated, as if he was savouring sweet nectar.

Jessica nearly laughed but managed to contain her hilarity.

Brian said, 'We've a lot to talk about, Patrick, and so we'd better get back and sort out the details.'

'Anything you say, Brian. Just lead the way.'

Even as they struggled back along the path, they were talking about tools. O'Rourke was telling Brian what tools and equipment would be needed. Some of the tools Jessica had never heard of, like an angle grinder, pumps, fountain heads, a bolster chisel, a mason's hammer and wire snips, to mention but a few. Other things were more common like spades and rakes, sledgehammers, trowels and a wheelbarrow.

'The thing is, Brian, with such a large area of land, you can have such a beautiful variety. Paths, steps, patios, ponds, pools and rockeries. Climbing plants can be not only colourful and beautiful, but useful as well. I always use a colour wheel.'

'A colour wheel?' Brian echoed. 'I've never heard of that.'

'The colour wheel or colour circle has colours arranged so that complementary colours fall opposite each other. I'll draw it for you and I'll be able to explain better when we get back to the village.'

'You certainly seem to know your job, Patrick. And I'm sure you'll do your best, even though Jessica and I won't be living here for a while.'

'You can trust me, Brian. I swear on my mother's grave you can trust me to work hard and do a good job.'

'Ponds, pools and rockeries, you say? It won't be easy to do that, will it? Difficult enough, I'd think, just to clear up the place so that we can comfortably walk through it up to the house.'

Patrick threw back his blond head and laughed.

'Oh Brian, I've already got wonderful ideas to transform the whole estate. The bare bones are there already, if you can see past the growth. I'll work on having it presentable first, but then we can work to transform the estate with modern ideas. You said you have children?'

'Yes, twins. A boy and a girl.'

'I'll make a sandpit and a wonderful play area for them.'

'Well, as I say, it might be a long time before they would be living here.'

Patrick shrugged. 'It'll take me quite a long time to do all the work needed. But one day . . . Oh, just you wait and see.'

Once they got back to Mrs Mellors' cottage, it was decided that Brian would take Patrick over to the Vale of Lennox Hotel across the Green, where they would have peace to talk away from any noise and interruptions from the children. Jessica noticed that O'Rourke was as charming and flattering to Tommy and Fiona as he had been to Mrs Peterson.

'What beautiful curls you have, Fiona,' he said, stroking her head, 'just like your beautiful Mammy. And Tommy, you have the straight hair of a man, like your Daddy. I think curls on a man are sissy, don't you?'

The children were charmed not only by his words but by his lilting Irish accent.

Jessica stayed with the children as she felt she had imposed on Mrs Mellors' time for long enough.

'We've been getting on fine, Jessie. I've been sitting here with my knitting while they've been messing about with these electronic games, or whatever they call them.'

'How's the knitting going?' Jessica asked. 'I could be making some things for you in Saudi and posting them on to you if you like. Although I don't know how dependable the post is there.'

'No, no. I always manage to keep the stall full. I must have the fastest knitting needles in Glasgow now. Although I do miss your sales patter, I admit. And your pretty face and curly hair attracted a lot of male customers.' She laughed. 'What they did with the baby stuff you persuaded them to buy, I'll never know.'

'Don't forget all the women's jerseys and things I sold too. Their wives and girlfriends would appreciate them.'

'Aye. Aye. But how are you getting on in that compound place, that's what I'd like to know? Now that we've a chance to talk without Brian being here, you can spill the beans.'

'It's really a wonderful life. I wish you could see the place, both inside the compound and outside in the desert. But I admit I'd rather be back in the Barras. Or even in Vale of Lennox.'

'Well, at least one of these days, you'll be back in the area if Brian does what he says and retires to Hilltop House. And of course I'm hoping you'll both spend more of his leaves here.'

'I hope so too. Brian said he'll eventually have the house painted to make it look more cheery but I can't see that being possible. The walls are all dark panelled wood. The only thing I can see being a possibility is new, brighter-coloured carpets.'

'Cream-coloured carpet all through,' Mrs Mellors suggested.

Jessica nodded. 'I suppose.'

'Anyway, you know you and the children would be welcome to stay here. My own family always come first, of course, but it's not likely they'd be here. My son and his wife and my three grandchildren have only been back all together once for a holiday from Australia since they've been away. They keep trying to persuade me to go over there – to stay for good with them or even just go for a few months. But you know me. I don't like to leave my stall and all my friends or my nice wee cottage here.' She sighed. 'My son's an awful good boy. He's been a few times back to see me despite the expense. He'd do anything for me, that boy.'

'Yes,' Jessica said. 'Anyone could see he's really fond of you.'

'I'll maybe get somebody to look after the stall and go over there for a month or two some time, just to please him.'

'So you should. I'm just wondering now how Brian's getting on with that Patrick O'Rourke. He's a right charmer, isn't he?'

'Mm.' Mrs Mellors looked thoughtful, making Jessica feel slightly uneasy.

15

At least the twins were happy and excited to be back in the compound. They loved the school and all the organised recreational activities after school hours. There was even a school holiday activity club. There were so many activities to choose from, and so far the children had learned to swim and had noisy fun in the pool most days. They played junior ping-pong and were even learning karate. They jumped up and down on a trampoline in the large air-conditioned sports hall. They enjoyed the many parties that were regularly organised for all the youngsters. Before Jessica had even unpacked their suitcase, Tommy and Fiona had raced away to join a crowd of other children.

In a few days, Brian organised a drive to Jordan and the spot near the Dead Sea where historians reckoned Jesus was baptised. They also managed a desert day-trip, but without the children.

'It's an awful nuisance, all the equipment we have to take,' Jessica complained.

'You don't know how dangerous the desert can be, darling. But we'll be all right as long as we have everything we might need.'

Actually she would far rather have gone to the tennis court and had a game of tennis or to one of the ladies' coffee mornings and enjoyed a coffee and a good blether. Or even just a walk. The compound was a good mile square and so there was plenty of scope for walking or jogging. But Brian was obviously enthusiastic about the day-trip across the desert.

They had already informed someone of their travel route. This was necessary, she supposed, in case they got lost or were attacked or God knew what else. Brian had also followed the rules in making sure his car was serviceable. He had to check wheels and tyres and spare tyre, jack, oil, fuel and water levels, and so on. They packed refreshments but no alcohol, of course. Saudi laws had to be strictly observed. Then there was the survival equipment in case of any emergency. Brian read the list out as Jessica helped to pack everything.

'25 litres of water per person, re-hydrate salts, spare blankets, spare petrol, shovel, compass, cigarette lighter or matches, torch, food, mobile phone, tow rope, knife, whistle . . .'

'For pity's sake,' Jessica gasped. 'There won't be enough room for us if we take any more stuff.'

'I think that should do.'

'Thank goodness.'

'Oh, and don't forget the sun cream we brought back from Glasgow.'

'OK. OK.' Then she giggled. 'It didn't half cause a bit of excitement with everybody when we brought back all that Marmite and Weetabix. Who would have thought it!'

'Darling,' he stopped Jessica from getting into the car. 'You'll have to wear your abaya. If someone saw you dressed like that, you'd be in trouble. Remember, you could be arrested and whipped.'

Jessica groaned. 'Who's likely to see me in the middle of the desert?'

'We'll be visiting various places.'

'I hate the bloody thing.'

'I thought you'd got used to it.'

'After being back home again and being able to wear whatever I fancied, it's murder having to be hidden all the time from top to toe.'

'I'm sorry, but you'd better get used to it again.'

Once out of the compound, Jessica said, 'By the way, you never told me everything about Patrick O'Rourke. Did you get properly organised? Did he agree to everything you wanted?'

'Yes. I'm not going to pay him much of a wage, to begin with at least. For one thing, he'll have board and lodging. And we'll see how he gets on. Although he certainly sounds as if he knows landscape gardening, right enough. I've arranged it all through the bank and the solicitor. The previous owner already had a financial arrangement set up for Mr and Mrs Peterson's wages and expenses. He was away from the house a lot on shoots, apparently.'

'That's obvious from the horrible trophies all round the walls. Once we settle there to live, I'm going to get rid of them. I don't want reminded every day about all those poor animals he killed.'

'Fair enough. I don't like the look of them either. We could try to find a few good paintings.'

'Bright-coloured ones. Some good modern paintings with bright, abstract colours.'

Brian smiled. 'Everything's going to be fine.'

'Aye, right,' Jessica said. All the same, she wished she was back home in Scotland, but not in Hilltop House. She was a Glasgow girl at heart, always had been and always would be. She no more wanted to settle in Hilltop House than in the middle of the desert. Often she still secretly longed for the Barras and her flat in the Calton. Despite what Mrs Mellors said about the Barras not being the cheery place it used to be.

'Remember the laughs we used to get at some of the patter?' Mrs Mellors had said. 'And you were in there doing your spiel with the best of them, even when you were a wee lassie helping your mammy on her stall.'

'Och, the Barras'll never change.'

'You're wrong, Jessie. They've changed all right. It's still an enormous market and of course, you can still get everything from a wee needle to a kitchen sink and bigger. But there's not the same cheery patter.'

Jessica wondered how Evie was getting on in the clinic and drop-in centre. How she admired the girl and the work she so willingly and generously did for what most people would regard as hopeless cases. Jessica had invited her to come out to the compound for a holiday and a rest. She had concentrated on telling Evie about the beautiful sunshine and all the wonderful facilities and social events in the compound. But Evie had refused the invitation.

'Too many of "my people" ', she said, 'urgently need me and depend on me in the Calton. I can't leave them.'

Jessica believed that Evie Jeffreys was the nearest thing to a saint that she'd come across or would ever be likely to come across. She'd once said as much to Evie and Evie had laughed.

'Don't be daft. I'm just doing my job, like everyone else. I'm not the only one who works here, in case you hadn't noticed.'

Nevertheless, Jessica believed Evie was the best of them all.

'I remember one time,' Brian was saying now, 'some of my Saudi friends invited me out to the desert for food and soft drinks. They slaughtered a sheep – halal style – and slowly baked it in a hole they had dug in the ground. The Saudi hospitality is always absolutely fantastic.'

Brian was always going on about his Saudi friends. He loved the people, the compound and the country as much as she loved the people of Glasgow, the Calton and Scotland. Sometimes she worried in case he might never want to leave the place. He was now talking happily about Tabuk's historical background being long and distinguished.

'The marks can still be seen today.'

'What marks?' Jessica hadn't been paying too much attention. Her mind had wandered back to Scotland.

'In the past, it served as a railway station on the Hejaz line until its destruction in World War One by Lawrence of Arabia. It's remained unrepaired ever since. But that's because of the development of road and air links.'

'I think I once saw a film about him.'

'Yes, I believe there was a film. Look, there's a desert dog! The Arabs consider it to be the finest dog in the world. Never try to approach one, though. They're wild animals.'

Jessica rolled her eyes. 'As if I'd come away out here to pat a dog.'

'Of course not, but they often loiter about near where any humans live, looking for food. Camels are different. They keep away from population centres.'

A few camels were making their leisurely way across the road in front of the car.

'I wish I could take you to two of the holiest cities in Saudi – Mecca and Medina. Hundreds of thousands of Muslims from all over the world make the pilgrimage to Mecca each year but entry into Mecca or Medina is prohibited to non-Muslims.'

'Good job then. I've not the slightest interest in going there.'

Brian sighed. 'Don't you feel the magic of the place yet, Jessica? It's such a marvellous country.'

'I can see you definitely think so.'

'But it is.'

'OK. OK.'

'Its people enjoy an enviable standard of living. It's one of the most politically stable and prosperous countries in the world.'

'OK, I said. I believe you. Honestly, I do. It's just that you keep going on about it so much.'

Brian shrugged. 'Sorry.'

After that, they concentrated on sightseeing and having a picnic. Eventually, they made their way back to the compound. Jessica felt exhausted, partly by the heat and partly by the long drive. She decided to have a quick plunge in the pool to cool down before going to the sports centre to collect the children. Brian drove round to his office building to prepare a few notes for the next day's schedule.

It was when she went to collect the children that she discovered to her shock and horror that there had been a terrorist attack on the compound earlier in the day.

'Now, there's no need to worry,' one of the teachers assured her. 'We took all the children into the school's panic room and the guards repulsed the terrorists and sent them packing in no time. The children thought it was great fun, an exciting adventure.'

Jessica was not comforted. Terrorist attacks, as far as she knew, always happened during the night. Never again would she be happy allowing Fiona and Tommy out of her sight.

'Honestly,' the teacher repeated, even laughing as she spoke. 'There's no need whatsoever to worry. You'll get used to it.'

Now Jessica was not so sure.

16

'You've got to stop being so neurotic about this.' Brian's voice had an edge of anger as well as impatience. 'You cannot go on coddling the twins and stopping their freedom to enjoy life here.'

'Neurotic?' Jessica gasped. 'You think I'm just imagining the danger they could be in? There was a terrorist attack, for God's sake. They could have been killed.'

'No, they could not. The terrorists never get through the gates. The guards always repulse them. I've been here for years and I know what I'm talking about. And you're forgetting the panic room. Once that iron wall comes down, nobody could possibly get in.'

'They're obviously getting worse when they're now attacking the place during the day.'

'Jessica, will you relax and just enjoy life here like you were doing before, and allow the children to enjoy life as they were doing before. Look at all the other children. They haven't let anything bother them. And don't forget about all the good teachers who are looking after the children so well.'

Jessica closed her eyes, bit her lip and then took a deep breath.

'OK. OK. I'll try.'

And so Tommy and Fiona went back to their school lessons and to racing about enjoying all the after-school activities.

Jessica went back to the café and began chatting to her friends there about her trip to Scotland. She described Hilltop House and its jungle of surrounding land and they gasped and shuddered at how eerie it all sounded. They giggled about the handsome and charming Irishman who was going to be living and working there.

'You'd better watch him, Jessica. He'll be making passes at you before you know what's happening. You'd probably enjoy it, though.'

'No way! I've a handsome husband, don't forget, and I'm madly in love with him. I don't need any Irish charmers.'

'Well,' one of the girls laughed, 'next time you go over there, take me with you and introduce me. I could do fine with an Irish charmer.'

'Once I settle there, you'll all be welcome to come and visit.'

She meant it. It was hard to imagine a gregarious person like herself being happy and feeling at home in such an isolated and wild-looking place. Of course, once Brian retired, he'd be with her and once they transformed the place into a hotel, it wouldn't be so isolated. It would be cheerful and interesting. She would be happy and content having him at her side. At the back of her mind, however, was always the worry that he'd never want to leave his excellent, very highly paid job and all the freebies he had at the compound. Then there was the obvious fact that he loved Saudi Arabia and all his Arab friends.

She could understand how he felt. Life in the compound (if you didn't consider the terrorist attacks) was truly wonderful. Even the climate was wonderful. There was an air of such happy excitement about the place with so many activities and social pleasures to look forward to each and every day.

She settled back into compound life and began thoroughly enjoying it again. They began entertaining quite a lot in their villa. She would have been happier preparing the food herself but, of course, with such an eager and conscientious Indian houseboy, she didn't stand a chance. She and Brian visited their friends' villas too. They played cards on the veranda and sipped long cool drinks of lemonade or orange juice. They didn't dare risk anything resembling alcohol, which was a bit of a nuisance, but it could literally cost you your life to flout any Muslim laws. They still could dream of double whiskies and tall glasses of frothy beer, however.

One night in bed, as he held Jessica lovingly in his arms, Brian said, 'Are you happy now, darling?'

'After being made love to like that – of course I'm happy.'

'Now, you know what I mean. Are you happy to be back in the compound and are you completely enjoying life here like you did before my last leave?'

'Yes, of course.'

'It's a truly wonderful life, isn't it?'

Again she felt a tweak of worry.

'Yes, it definitely is, Brian. Nobody could deny that. But you will retire eventually, won't you? I mean, you will move back with me and the twins to Scotland eventually?'

'Of course. But that's a long way off yet. Meantime, we'll spend at least some of my leaves there because we'd be best to keep in touch with how Patrick O'Rourke's getting on.'

She was glad of the regular correspondence she had with Mrs Mellors and Evie. They thought she was really lucky to be living in what sounded like such a wonderful place. She had, of course, described in her letters to them the compound, the climate and all the exciting social life, and she believed she really was lucky. It was just the idea of being there forever that worried her. She couldn't help it. There were still times when she missed Glasgow.

Mrs Mellors' son had been over to visit her in Vale of Lennox and was still trying to persuade her to go over to Australia – at least for a few months, to begin with.

'I've promised that I'll go over. It's just a case of deciding when,' Mrs Mellors wrote.

Jessica hoped she wouldn't disappear away to Australia when she and Brian came to live in Hilltop House. Mrs Mellors had been like a mother to her since her own mother died. And a friendly, protective one at that. No doubt her visit to Australia would be long past before she and Brian settled in Hilltop House.

The next day Brian started talking about a trip to the beach.

'Oh, the children will love that,' Jessica said.

'No, we can't take the children.'

'Why on earth not?'

'Well, for one thing they might take their shoes off and even with them on, they could get cut on the razor-sharp coral. Then there's the spiny sea urchins and the highly poisonous stonefish.'

'Charming!'

'You know they love doing everything in the compound. They never want to go outside of it.'

Now she wasn't fussy about a beach trip. As usual, however, Brian was brimming over with enthusiasm and so she tried to share his pleasant anticipation.

Admittedly, once they reached the beach, she truly did enjoy the experience. The scenery was out of this world. The turquoise blue sea shimmered into the distance, the sand sparkled as if it was strewn with diamonds as minute particles of silica reflected the brazen sun. A cool breeze, redolent of ozone, wafted shorewards.

'I told you,' Brian said, 'how beautiful it would be. I knew you'd enjoy it.'

She gave him a loving hug.

'You're far too good for me. And patient as well. I don't deserve you.'

He kissed the tip of her nose.

'I adore you. Always have done and always will.'

They enjoyed a leisurely drive back and went to the café for a bite to eat before going in search of the children to take them home. Brian said he would drive to his office and do an hour's work before joining them at the villa. After they enjoyed a coffee and a snack, off Brian went and she stayed for another cup of coffee and a chat with some of her friends out on the café veranda.

Some of the others also had children to collect. One of them said, 'I always find it's a devil of a job trying to drag them away. They're always having such a wonderful time. Sometimes, I think they get over-excited with it all.'

'What have they been up to today, I wonder?' Jessica asked.

'I think the teachers were taking them on a walk to the furthest away bits of the compound that they haven't seen before.'

'At least that should tire them out,' Jessica said, 'and they'll get a good sleep tonight.'

Eventually, they all waved goodbye to each other and made for their own villas, except for a couple of the women who did part-time work at the café and who started clearing up the tables.

Jessica decided to go down to the school to check if the children were back yet. She also tried the sports centre. Both places were empty of children. She went to the villa. As usual, there was nothing to do there. Everything was spick and span and not a thing out of place that she could tidy up. The houseboy was so irritatingly efficient.

Then suddenly the siren howled a warning. A terrorist attack had started. Jessica raced outside.

'The children. The children.'

She was not the only one who was crying out the words in panic.

17

Suicide bombers flung themselves at the gate, blowing up the barrier and the barbed wire.

Two Mercedes saloons rocketed forward into the gap, as wisps of smoke and dust covered the bodies of the Saudi guards, the blood strangely brown and moist as the dust coated and disguised the horror of the broken flesh.

The tyres slammed and bumped over the rubble and torn bodies and burst through to the Stepford-like streets of middle American suburbia.

Women in pretty flowered tea dresses dashed to and fro incongruously between swarthy uniformed Saudis.

The two Mercedes diverged left and right, the heavy clatter of machine guns beating a staccato tattoo of destruction. There was a smell of burning rubber, mingled with the stench of cordite, as the tyres struggled for grip on the hot tarmac.

Bullets sprayed in every direction, making a 'thock thock' sound as they slammed into the concrete walls. Interspersed with this was the heavy meaty thud as bullets ripped into guards and civilians alike.

In horror, Jessica saw one of her friends from the café throw up her arms before crashing back on to the ground. Blood was cascading from the back of her neck. Jessica pressed herself against the wall of the villa. She might have slid round and in through the back door. On the other hand, how could she hide safely away, knowing that the children were outside and in immediate danger? But what could she do to help them? The only thing she could think of was to get to them in time to warn them to turn back and hide. But how could she accomplish this? She was almost too afraid to breathe in case one of the terrorists saw her.

Brian would be safely in his office panic room and so she didn't need to worry about him. But oh, the children, the children.

They too would be shot and killed. Even if the terrorists had mercy for children, the danger would still remain of them being caught in the crossfire in the blinding smoke. Jessica was in hell. She felt hysterical. The smoke, the overpowering noise fuelled by hatred, the fires. Buildings were crackling with flames.

Paralysed now, she couldn't move. She believed her death was very near.

Heavy machine guns from the towers finally sighted on the cars and a terrible crossfire of bullets tore through the metal of the cars, destroying everything and everyone inside. The sudden absence of sound was in strange contrast to the ringing in Jessica's ears as she stared wide-eyed in stunned paralysis at the devastation around her. Dust and smoke partially blanked the scene as dazed, zombie-like figures staggered aimlessly, seemingly unsure if they were alive or in some nightmare.

Now when she opened her eyes, she could see dead bodies. She began to sob and cry. She didn't know how long she stood like that before Brian came racing towards her, caught her in his arms and led her into the villa.

'Darling,' he said, sitting her down on a chair. 'I thought you were safely in the panic room. God, what I'd give for a couple of stiff whiskies but we'll just have to make do with a cup of tea.'

As if the words were magic, the houseboy suddenly appeared and cried out, 'Me make tea' before rushing off to the kitchen.

'The children,' Jessica managed. 'I wanted to get to the children and warn them.'

'Good God! Weren't they in the school panic room?'

'No, the teachers had taken them out on a walk to explore the far end of the compound.'

'Where are they now?'

'I hope and pray they're still at the other end of the compound. Probably the teachers heard the noise of all the gunfire and kept them there. But we'll have to go and find them.' She struggled to her feet. 'Right now.'

The sights outside the villa made her feel sick but she ran through the dust and dead bodies, shouting at Brian, 'You go that way and I'll try this side. Hurry, for God's sake.'

It didn't take too long, although it seemed like an eternity, before she found the children and their teachers safe and sound. She stopped, almost fainting with relief but worried then about what to do next.

Tommy and Fiona started happily chattering to her. Tommy said, 'We saw lots of lovely trees and flowers and shrubs and Miss Donaldson said there's a small army of Indian, Bangladeshi and South-East Asian workers who keep the gardens looking great like that.'

'Wonderful,' Jessica murmured. She was still practising taking deep breaths to calm herself. She kept glancing over at the teachers too. So far they had protected all the children from the horrors of what had happened. But what to do now?

Fiona said, 'Miss Smithers told us that outside in the desert, there's just scrubland and some coarse grass. A tree called the spiny acacia grows along dry river beds and seems to survive everything. It's all the workers that keep everything inside the compound so lovely and green and colourful.'

Tommy said, 'We got quite tired, Mummy. Because we enjoyed ourselves so much. We didn't come straight back because Miss Donaldson said we'd be best to stay for a while and rest. We were away for ages. I fell asleep.'

'So did I,' Fiona said. 'In a beautiful flowery place with high bushes all around. Miss Grayley told us to lie down. There was nobody could see us and disturb us and we'd have a really good sleep.' She giggled. 'All the teachers crouched down beside us. They looked funny.'

'You're lucky to have such good teachers,' Jessica said, then hesitated before plunging on. 'They saved your lives, you see – all of your lives. Now you've got to be brave. There has been a terrible terrorist attack on the compound – really terrible. Lots of people have been wounded and killed. It's perfectly safe again now and the soldiers have killed the terrorists but there are some horrid sights. We'll have to pass through lots of horrid things before we can get back home.'

Just then, other mothers and fathers came running to join them and snatch their children into their arms. Cries of 'Thank God you're safe' echoed all round in the hot desert air. Brian appeared too and said to Jessica, 'Now calm down. They're safe and well. That's the main thing.'

She suddenly felt an almost overwhelming urge to punch him.

'I'll carry Fiona and hide her face against my shoulder to try and stop her seeing anything. You do the same for Tommy.'

'You can't carry Fiona, Jessica. Some things have to be faced. It's life. The children have got to learn to be strong. We'll hold their hands and lead them. They can close their eyes if they feel they need to.'

Jessica began to tremble. If it hadn't been for the now crowds of other parents and teachers all milling around, she would have screamed.

'Keep calm,' he was saying again. 'Set the children a good example.'

She managed to control herself and lead the children back towards the villa, as he said. She did keep calm even when the children began to sob and cry and hide their faces against her and Brian.

At long last they reached the house and did everything possible to soothe and comfort the twins before tucking them into bed. Jessica sat beside their trembling bodies until eventually, exhausted, they sank into sleep.

By then she was too exhausted herself and too emotionally drained to be angry.

She said to Brian, 'Those teachers obviously saved the children's lives.'

'Yes,' Brian agreed. 'I've always admired their conscientiousness, as well as their considerable talents.'

'Was it you who engaged them originally?'

'Yes.'

'You're obviously good at your job, Brian. But you didn't think the terrorists would ever get past the Saudi soldiers, did you?'

Brian shrugged. 'I've been here for years, as I've told you, and it's never happened before.'

'Well, it happened today and it'll happen again.'

'We don't know that.'

'Brian, the terrorists have proved to themselves and to everyone that they can get in. Of course they'll try again. They'll think that all they'll need is more men and no doubt they'll have plenty of men eager to join them.'

'We'll get more soldiers stationed all around the walls. That'll stop them.'

'You hope.'

'There just weren't enough soldiers on duty today, Jessica. That'll be put right. You've no need to worry.'

'How many times have you said that to me, Brian? I've lost count. But one thing's certain. I'll never be happy here again.'

'Oh Jessica, please don't say that. This has been an awful day for you, I know, but you'll feel better tomorrow and everything will soon be back to normal.'

Jessica shook her head.

'No.'

'Yes, darling. You're happy here. Everyone is. It's such a wonderful place and . . .'

'I know. You don't need to say it. It's a wonderful compound, a wonderful country, and Arabs are wonderful people.'

'Well, it's true, isn't it?'

'It's true for you.'

'Jessica, I don't believe there is a single person who has lived here for any length of time who would disagree with me.'

'Are you actually saying that it will be all right for our children to go on living here after what happened today? After how traumatised they've been?'

'Today was a one-off. It won't happen again, and you're forgetting how happy our children have been here. Living here has been a wonderful experience for them. They're very, very lucky.'

'Lucky to be alive.'

'Oh, stop it, Jessica. You've always been such an extremist.'

'I don't care any more what you think. I want to take the children home.'

'This is their home.'

'Not any more. It has to be Hilltop House from now on.'

'Don't be ridiculous.' Brian's voice turned angry. 'Hilltop House isn't habitable yet and it's sheer selfishness on your part to even consider taking the children from their enjoyable life here to that dark jungle of a place, as it is at the moment.'

'I'll stay with Mrs Mellors if necessary until Hilltop House is habitable. I'm just not staying here any longer, Brian.'

18

'Please darling. I promise you, if you still want to go to Hilltop House, I'll agree wholeheartedly, but just give me this chance first. I'm sure you'll feel better after a holiday – especially a holiday in such a wonderful place as Dubai. The children will love it too and it'll do them so much good, as well as you.'

He kissed her.

'Please. My Arab friend has given us the use of his flat and I've managed to get a week's compassionate leave.'

He had been going on at her so much that eventually, for the sake of peace, she agreed.

As it turned out, it was an experience she would not have missed for the world. It was, in fact, like another world. To get to the district where Brian's Arab friend's flat was situated, they had to take a water taxi. The flat, as Brian had once told her, was absolutely enormous and unbelievably luxurious. She couldn't help feeling, though, that it was too much over the top. Who needed anything so large? But then, she soon discovered that everything in Dubai was huge. In one street there was a mix of hotels and business premises with buildings sixty floors high. Other streets had even taller buildings. One building, Brian told her, was the tallest in the world. New buildings were sprouting up everywhere from unfinished roads. There were harbours crowded with fishing boats. Other harbours boasted luxurious yachts.

Everywhere she looked there were beautiful, marble-floored shopping malls with the most wonderful shops Jessica had ever seen. Designer labels were everywhere and jewellery she had never even been able to dream about. In one mall, there was a glass wall the whole length of the place and in behind the glass was an aquarium – but no ordinary aquarium. There were all sorts of fish – even sharks – and marine life. The children stared pop-eyed and open-mouthed.

Brightly coloured toys sent them screaming in delight. They rode rocking horses and drove racing cars until Jessica had to insist they went to find somewhere to sit down and calm down.

They found an ice cream parlour with every kind of ice cream imaginable. The children rolled their eyes and sighed with pleasure.

Brian said to Jessica, 'Now do you believe me? They're fine already. What happened before will just be like a bad dream and will fade away and be completely forgotten. By the look of things, it's forgotten already.'

She could see what he meant and, as far as the children were concerned, he could be right. Children could be very resilient. However, she couldn't forget what had happened in the compound and how near they had all come to a horrible, violent death. She could also think ahead and know that, despite all of Brian's assurances, it could happen again. She was having a wonderful experience in Dubai, of course, and enjoying it. She did not regret allowing Brian to persuade her to visit the place. She felt lucky to have had such an opportunity. She realised too that Brian was trying his best to help her and the twins and he genuinely believed such a serious terrorist attack would never happen again.

There would be extra soldiers put on duty, no doubt, as he said. But she believed there would be more terrorists too. There was bound to be the revenge element, for one thing. So many of the terrorists had been killed. Despite every assurance

Brian gave her, she thought it would be absolute madness to remain in the compound in Saudi Arabia.

Her dearest wish would be for Brian to come home to Scotland with her and the twins and stay there permanently. They could work together on the hotel project and be busy and happy. But she couldn't see Brian agreeing to that. She did suggest it but, as she expected, Brian said that there would be plenty of time for that eventually, but he had such a wonderfully well-paid job in the compound and it was such a wonderful life for her and the twins. Wonderful, wonderful! Everything was wonderful in the compound, in Tabuk, everywhere in Saudi Arabia. And, of course, the people – he never tired of singing their praises.

The only reason his attitude did not make her really angry was the memory that she had once done the very same to him about the Barras, the Calton, Glasgow and Scotland.

She sighed to herself. What a pair they were – both so extreme in their ideas. Maybe that was one of the reasons she loved Brian so much. She understood him. In so many ways, he was so like herself.

That night, in the enormous football pitch of a bedroom, she lay awake in his arms after he had made passionate love to her. She listened to the soft regularity of his breathing. He was now enjoying a peaceful sleep, happy in the thought, no doubt, that she had been persuaded to stay, and would now return with him to the compound and remain there with him.

She wanted to be with him. But nothing had changed her mind. A terrible sadness engulfed her. She tried to fight her way out of it by reminding herself that Brian could come over to Scotland and spend every leave with her and the children. She fell asleep eventually but when she woke up next morning, the depression still lay heavy on her. She made every effort to hide it and sound cheerful.

Brian was telling the children, 'You get eucalyptus trees and date trees in parks here. And lots of animals like the striped hyena, the desert fox, the Arabian oryx. And birds like the houbara bustard and the falcon. In the waters here, there are more than three hundred species of fish.'

He told her, 'There are a lot of festivals and entertainments we can come back and enjoy. Every month there's something. In January and February, there's the Marathon and the Shopping Festival. In March, there's the Jazz Festival and the tennis championship. In April . . .'

'OK. OK.' Jessica had to stop him before he went through the whole year. 'I believe you. There's lots going on.'

He chatted happily to the twins most of the way back from Dubai until, exhausted with all their adventures, the children fell asleep.

The compound had, thankfully, been cleaned up. There was no sign of the bloody carnage they had left.

'Are you glad to be home?' Brian asked, giving her a loving hug. She could hardly believe her ears. He actually believed that the cleaning-up process and the holiday in Dubai had changed everything, including her mind.

The houseboy had kept the villa looking immaculate and immediately rushed to make them tea as soon as they put a foot inside the house. The children had looked anxious and had clung to her as soon as they entered the compound and so she knew the memory of the earlier horrors were still at the back of their minds. A week's holiday wasn't long enough to completely eradicate the memory. Brian had to rush back to catch up with work in his office and by the time he returned, the children were in bed and fast asleep.

Brian said confidently, 'They'll be fine. Once they get back to school and start enjoying all their after-school activities again.'

Jessica sighed. 'Brian, I'm sorry. I meant what I said and I haven't changed my mind. I can't stay here any longer. I'm taking the children back to Scotland.'

'But darling, you can't . . .'

Jessica bristled. 'You can't force me to stay here. I'm going, I said, and nothing you can say or do is going to stop me.'

He sighed. 'I know. And of course I won't force you. And we'll be together on each and every one of my leaves. But what I was going to say was that you can't go just now because I can't go with you just now. I've had word from the Saudi government and I need to attend an important meeting with them. It's miles away and . . .'

'I can manage by myself. Don't worry.'

'Darling, are you sure?'

'Of course. I'm sorry it's got to be like this, Brian. You know I love you and want to be with you. But I'll look forward to you coming over and being with me and the children on your next leave.'

And so it was decided that she'd go right away and stay with Mrs Mellors until she felt that Hilltop House was habitable.

19

There was no answer at Mrs Mellors' door. Jessica wondered if she'd be across at the shop on the Green. She wasn't there either. As a last resort, she led the children along Abercromby Street to the doctor's surgery.

Mrs Plockton must have seen her from an upstairs window because the other windows looked out to either the back of the house or the sides.

'Hello, my dear girl. And these must be your lovely little ones. Come in. Come in. Pinkie has someone in the surgery just now but you're welcome here in my house any time.' She led them through into the sitting room.

'Actually,' Jessica said, 'I was just wanting to enquire about Mrs Mellors. She's all right, I hope. She's usually at home during the week, knitting stock for her stall, but she doesn't seem to be in and I've looked around everywhere.'

Mrs Plockton covered her mouth with her hand in a dramatic gesture, then she said, 'She's gone.'

'Gone? What do you mean?'

'My poor dear girl. Didn't you get her letter telling you?'

'No.'

'Well, that's very strange. Very strange indeed.'

'Not really. The mail's terrible in the compound. It takes ages to get there.'

'Oh well, it should be there when you get back.'

'I'm not going back.'

'Oh, you poor dear. Your marriage has broken down.'

'No, it hasn't.' Jessica tried to keep the intense irritation out of her voice. 'I've just decided to live here from now on and my husband's going to spend every leave with me. He'll be coming over in a couple of weeks' time.'

'He wouldn't come with you today?'

'He couldn't come with me today. He had some pre-arranged meetings with people from the Saudi government. He had to travel to the other end of the country to see them.'

'Well, of course,' Mrs Plockton sighed, 'if that's what was important to him.'

Jessica could have punched her. Like everyone else, she felt sorry for poor Dr Plockton who was stuck in the same house with her. And fancy calling him Pinkie. She continued to use the stupid name at every opportunity.

'What was in Mrs Mellors' letter?' Jessica had no doubt that Mrs Plockton had in her special sneaky way got the information out of Mrs Mellors.

'She's gone to Australia for a few months to stay with her son.' Mrs Plockton's voice lowered confidentially. 'But if you ask me, she'll never come back. She adores her son. She won't want to leave him ever again.'

Jessica could have wept. Mrs Plockton was now handing out sweeties to the children, who had been sitting quietly, one on each side of Jessica on the settee.

'What good little darlings,' Mrs Plockton was saying to them. 'And didn't you like it over in that nasty compound? You poor things.' She shook her head sadly. 'Now you'll have to live in that horrid Hilltop House.' Her voice lowered. 'I've heard there's a ghost up there.'

Jessica jumped up.

'How dare you try to frighten the children! Come on.' She dragged the twins away.

'She's a very bad woman. Don't you listen to her.'

Once outside she walked quickly to get away from the place but also to stop herself from breaking down and weeping.

Mrs Plockton ran part of the way after her, crying out, 'My dear girl. It was just my little joke.' Her voice was carried away in the wind now howling around the trees on the Green. Jessica crossed over on to Cruachan Road and slowed down as she walked in the direction of the Campsie Hills.

Every now and again she had to stop and rest, partly because the twins had become fractious and were complaining about being tired and having sore feet. Once on the 'jungle road', as she and Brian had come to refer to it, she was pleasantly surprised. Obviously Patrick O'Rourke had at least started on his clearing-up process. The path was quite easy to walk on now. For one thing, it was clear of ivy. Overhanging branches of trees and shrubs had been severely cut back. Although she still didn't think a car would be able to manoeuvre up the road, it was a bit of a relief to see some improvement. Maybe being here wasn't going to be so difficult after all. And once they had it up and running as a hotel, it would be, she imagined, a very popular place. That would make it more cheery.

Nevertheless, it took ages to get even within sight of Hilltop House and she had never been so glad to see anyone in her life as she was when Patrick O'Rourke suddenly appeared.

'Jessica!' he cried out with pleasure. 'And the beautiful twins. What a lovely surprise.'

Jessica could hardly speak, she was so tired. 'I don't think the twins are able to walk another step. They're absolutely exhausted.'

'Come to Patrick, my precious ones. Heave ho and off we go.' He swung them both into his arms and began marching the rest of the way towards the house, singing as he went. 'Jack and Jill went up the hill . . .' The twins began to giggle and then laugh out loud as he bounced them up and down to the rhythm of the song.

Jessica felt like laughing too. She certainly felt a lot better now at the thought of living in Hilltop House until Brian came to join her. It was only a couple of weeks, after all, and then he'd be with her for a month's leave. Then she'd have every leave after that to look forward to. And each time they would get some way further on with their plans to turn the house into a hotel.

The housekeeper, Mrs Peterson, must have heard them, because she was waiting to welcome them at the front door.

'Isn't Patrick making a good job of the path?' she said a few minutes later as she poured out a cup of tea for Jessica and gave the children some Irn Bru.

'Gosh yes. What a difference!'

Patrick said, 'I've hardly started on it. It needs to be much wider and it's a long distance to cover.' He flashed her one of his delightful smiles. 'Or rather uncover. But I'll get there. I'm a very patient and determined man.'

He was a very handsome man too, Jessica thought, and nearly asked him why he was still single. She decided it would be too cheeky and nosey to ask such a thing. She could just imagine Brian telling her to mind her own business and the man's private life didn't matter as long as he did the job they were paying him for.

Patrick was making faces at the children now and making them laugh again. Mrs Peterson passed around little iced fairy cakes she'd baked and Jessica complimented her on how delicious they were.

'Oh, she's a wizard of a woman,' Patrick said. 'Geordie's a very lucky man, aren't you Geordie? If she didn't belong to him, I'd be going down on my bended knee right now and proposing to her.'

'Aye well, she does,' Geordie growled. 'And don't you forget it.'

Mrs Peterson shook her head. 'For goodness sake, Geordie. The man's only joking.'

'Aye well, as long as he concentrates on his gardening and doesn't let his eyes wander on to anything else.'

Jessica felt quite cheerful after the tea and cakes.

'I'm sure you'll do a great job, Patrick. I knew that long road up here would take ages. And it needs to get done before you can tackle anywhere else on the grounds. But I've every confidence that you'll be able to manage it all.'

'Thank you, dear beautiful lady. I assure you I will never let you down. Never, never . . .'

Geordie got up from the table.

'You'd make anyone want to puke.'

'Geordie!' Mrs Peterson cried out angrily as he stomped away. 'Come back here and apologise.'

But Geordie didn't come back. Jessica supposed the man was just jealous of Patrick, especially if Patrick kept being so charming and flattering to his wife. And now to her too. She just felt amused by it. As far as she was concerned, he was a bit of a pain in the neck but good for a laugh at the same time. And in this dark-panelled, gloomy-looking house, anything that cheered the place up was a good thing. Although even the panelling might be an attraction to future hotel customers. She supposed the panelling was part of the unusual character of the place.

Eventually Mrs Peterson showed Jessica to the large room that was to be her bedroom. Jessica insisted, however, that the twins had to be with her.

'Will I bring in another bed?' Mrs Peterson asked.

'No, no. That bed's big enough for a dozen folk. Don't worry, it'll be fine, but thanks all the same.'

It was a huge four-poster with a tapestry roof and curtains all around.

'I'll serve dinner at six o'clock this evening in the dining room. Or whenever you wish. Just tell me what you'd prefer.'

'To be honest, I'd prefer just eating with you and Geordie, and Patrick, in the kitchen until my husband comes to stay. We can use the dining room while he's here.'

'Very well. You'll be welcome to join us then at six o'clock.'

'Thank you, Mrs Peterson. You're very kind.'

But in the long night after dinner? What then?

20

Every night Geordie sat by the kitchen fire smoking his pipe and reading a book or listening to the radio. Mrs Peterson, Patrick, Jessica and the twins played card games or Monopoly.

After a couple of nights, Jessica said, 'I'd better take the twins down to Vale of Lennox, introduce them to the head teacher and register them for school.'

Mrs Peterson said, 'There's only one teacher, a Mr Douglas Brown. He's a good teacher, I've heard. He lives in the schoolhouse and has only about a dozen primary pupils like Tommy and Fiona. Once they're eleven they'll have to travel further afield to one of the big schools.'

'One thing's for sure, I'm not going to trail them back and forward up that road at lunch times.'

'Oh, you won't need to,' Mrs Peterson assured her. 'All the children take a packed lunch and Mr Brown makes a pot of tea. They sit around his table and eat their lunch with him. I've heard that all the children adore him, so don't worry. The twins will be all right.'

'Well, that's a relief. I'll only need to walk down in the morning and then in the afternoon to collect them.'

'Mr Brown has a car. Once the road's widened and passable, he'll probably take the children home. The rest of his pupils live in Vale of Lennox, near enough the schoolhouse, so he doesn't need to worry about getting them home. But at the moment, of course, he couldn't get a car up that road.'

'He sounds a nice man.'

Jessica could hardly make herself heard above the squeals of hilarity from Tommy and Fiona, who were playing a card game with Patrick O'Rourke. It was high time the children were back at school and getting a bit of discipline again, as well as lessons.

The next day was a Saturday but Mrs Peterson assured Jessica that Douglas Brown would be there. So first thing next morning, she set off with the children. She was quickly caught up by Patrick, however. He appeared with a wheelbarrow, lifted the children into it and began racing with them down the road, much to their renewed hilarity. Jessica was finding it difficult to keep up with them and was glad (and breathless) when they reached Cruachan Road and Patrick waved goodbye to them. The schoolhouse was in Thorn Avenue, at the other side of the Green. It was a pretty cottage with a large extension containing a schoolroom, a kitchen with table and chairs, a toilet, and lots of deep cupboards which held maps and all sorts of teaching equipment.

Douglas Brown was a big man with hair as black as Brian's but he hadn't Brian's wonderful tan.

He warmly welcomed the children and showed them, as well as Jessica, all around. He gave the children access to one cupboard full of toys and games while he spoke to Jessica.

'I try to make the lessons as interesting and enjoyable as I can for all the children in my care,' he told Jessica. 'I have nature study, for instance, and we go out for walks to study the natural world around us. So it's not just a case of the three Rs.'

'I'm sure they'll be very happy at your school,' Jessica said. 'And it'll be all right if they eat their packed lunch here, will it?'

'Of course. You're living in Hilltop House, did you say?'

'Yes, it's a terrible long walk for them. That's the only disadvantage.'

'Don't worry. I have a car. It'll take me no time and it'll be no trouble to drive the children home after school.'

'That's terribly kind of you. I'd really appreciate it, Mr Brown. Unfortunately, at the moment, a car couldn't get up the road to the house. But I've a man working on it just now. It'll be passable eventually. I'll let you know when it's ready.'

'Well, rest assured, Mrs Anderson. Tommy and Fiona will be all right here. How about them getting here, though?'

She smiled. 'The man I mentioned who's working on the road is a bit of a joker. Patrick O'Rourke's his name and he's very good with the children. He wheeled them all the way down the hill in his wheelbarrow, much to their hilarity, as you can imagine. And the walk is good, healthy exercise for me.'

'That's fine then. So I'll expect them on Monday morning.'

'Yes.'

She collected the children and Douglas Brown showed them out.

'I'm sorry I can't help you home in any way just now,' he said. 'I'm meeting someone in Glasgow and I'm a bit late as it is.'

'Oh, I'm so sorry for keeping you back. Don't worry about us. It's a lovely day and we'll just take our time. Probably we'll meet up with Patrick again anyway.'

They waved goodbye and afterwards Jessica said to the children, 'Did you like Mr Brown?'

'Yes, he's great,' they cried out as they went skipping happily ahead of her. 'Will Patrick be there to give us another ride in his barrow, Mummy?'

'I expect so.'

Sure enough, they had only gone a few yards along the path when Patrick appeared, hoisted the twins into his wheelbarrow and started racing up the road. Jessica took her time. She told herself yet again that the exercise would be good for her. She wished all the same that she could have stayed with Mrs Mellors in the village until Brian arrived. Now she'd no choice. Once again, she thought with painful nostalgia of the flat in the Barras market. OK, Angus McDavie had desperately needed a place for him and his wife and family to live and the flat had been ideal for him, being so near his stall. Near enough too for his wife (pregnant yet again) and children to help him. Everyone had persuaded her, and the McDavies had pleaded with her to sell the flat to them. She had hung on to the flat for as long as she could, but realised eventually that it was a bit selfish of her to keep it lying empty.

As Mrs Mellors had said, 'Their need is greater than yours, Jessie. You've got Hilltop House and once you eventually transform it into a hotel, it'll be wonderful. Until then, you'll always have a home with me if you want it. Why would you want to be living in a flat in the Calton on your own ever again?'

'OK, OK,' she'd capitulated and eventually Angus and his brood had bought the flat.

Thinking of Mrs Mellors so far away in Australia made tears well up in her eyes. She swallowed down the lump in her throat and wiped her eyes with the back of her hand. She'd just have to look forward to the time that Mrs Mellors would return. Much as she knew the older woman loved her son, she couldn't imagine her leaving Scotland and especially her stall in the Barras for ever.

Hilltop House loomed up in front of Jessica – black against the blue of the sky. She experienced a sudden surge of hatred for the place. Struggling to control it, she told herself that once Brian was there and they began all the exciting plans they were going to put in motion, and he was sharing her bed, she'd feel differently about everything. As it was, despite being exhausted with all the walking she was doing, she hadn't been able to sleep. She had lain in the darkness of the panelled room listening to creakings and squeaking and the sad howl of the wind.

She decided that if she suffered one more night of sleeplessness, she'd be forced to go to Dr Plockton for some sleeping pills. She didn't relish having to put up with his ghastly mother again but she desperately needed the doctor's help. Maybe Mrs Plockton wouldn't be there. However, she'd heard that the awful woman was always there, interfering not only with the patients' lives but also with the treatment the doctor was trying to give them. Sometimes he had to be very firm and then she'd cry out for anyone to hear:

'Pinkie, Pinkie, you mustn't bully your poor mother. You mustn't let that red hair of yours give you such a bad temper. Naughty Pinkie . . .'

Not for the first time Jessica, and she was sure all of his patients, worried about him snapping altogether and murdering his mother. Nobody would blame him. Everyone felt like murdering her at some time or another. But they didn't want him to end up in jail.

Yet again, Jessica suffered a long night of fearful wakefulness and was forced, once she left the children at school, to make her way along Thorn Avenue and round on to Abercromby Street. As usual, of course, it was Mrs Plockton who opened the door and ushered her inside.

'Oh, my dear girl, are the little ones too much for you? You look so tired and pale and drained. Children can be so difficult. I know what it's like with Pinkie . . .'

'My children are not too much for me,' Jessica interrupted firmly. 'They attend school, enjoy being there and I'm happy for them. I came to see Dr Plockton on another matter.'

Just then, Dr Plockton's surgery door opened and he ushered an elderly lady out.

'Thank you so much for your help, doctor,' the old lady said. Dr Plockton smiled as he gently took her arm and led her to the outside door.

'Don't forget to put that prescription into the chemist's right away.'

'Yes, I'll go right now. Thanks again, doctor.'

Dr Plockton turned to Jessica. 'Can I help you?'

Mrs Plockton said, 'I was just saying to Mrs Anderson . . .'

'Can I come in and speak to you, doctor?' Jessica interrupted.

'Yes, do come right in.'

'I'll bring you in a cup of tea, my dear,' Mrs Plockton said.

'No thank you,' Jessica said firmly. 'I do not want tea. I just want to speak to the doctor in private.' She followed him in but not before she caught the flash of hatred that he aimed at his mother.

21

Jessica passed the time on most days while the children were at school by exploring the surrounding districts and reading up about their history. Lennoxtown used to have Lennox Castle, for instance. It was partly a general hospital, partly maternity, but mostly for people who were educationally subnormal, or what would be called nowadays people with learning difficulties. People in that part of the hospital usually remained there all of their lives. That's where unmarried girls who had babies and who later had their babies taken away from them were confined for a lifetime.

The castle was now an empty ruin and apparently Celtic football team had a training ground nearby.

The Lennoxes of Lennox Castle were lineally descended from Duncan, the eighth Earl of Lennox of the old line. He was beheaded in Stirling when he was eighty years of age. His son-in-law Murdoch and Murdoch's two sons were all executed on the same day.

Robert Burns knew what he was talking about when he wrote 'Man's inhumanity to man . . .'. All down the ages, there seem to have been the most appalling cruelties. In Scotland especially, there seemed to be some shocking excesses. Jessica had long ago read about Scotland being a hard-drinking country. She had in her reading, though, discovered that

Robert Burns did not like to drink. Alcohol upset his stomach. It was a terrible problem to him how so many people wanted to raise too many glasses to toast his success. The problem arose when they pressed him to raise too many glasses as well. But he avoided it whenever possible.

It interested Jessica to find out that up till about 1832 the workers in Lennoxtown were paid on a Saturday in public houses in the village. A room was given to the foreman where he could divide out the wages and it was expected that everyone in the room would spend something 'for the good of the house'.

It was this system that encouraged drinking to excess in Lennoxtown and probably in other Scottish places as well. A great many of the workmen spent too much of their hard-earned money before they left.

One man in the area, John Young, made a study of the geology of the Campsie area and formed a collection of its various rocks and fossils. As a result, Glasgow University put him in charge of the Hunterian Museum.

Jessica enjoyed finding out about all the places that were now part of her home area, as Glasgow had once been. A long time ago now, it seemed, she had enjoyed learning all about the history of Glasgow. She'd given Brian pleasure and interest in showing him around and telling him all about the different areas of Glasgow. Now she'd be able to do the same for him about the Campsie area.

She even took a notebook and a pen out with her to jot down some interesting facts in case she forgot them. More recent news to report to Brian was that the Campsie Glen area could be quite dangerous, and only the other day there had been an accident with a climber having to be rescued after falling down a gully. The Scottish Ambulance Service had been called out to help in the rescue and also a Navy Sea King helicopter. She found the days passed quickly and quite enjoyably. It was the nights in Hilltop House that she never could look forward to. The large gloomy bedroom depressed her, as did the four-poster bed with its drapes that gave off a peculiar fusty smell. It was the smell of age, Jessica thought. The whole place and everything in it was obviously ancient – except in the kitchen. As well as the oven next to the open coal fire, there was a modern cooker and also a microwave and a fridge freezer.

'It was when Mr Nairn had people here for the shoots,' Mrs Peterson explained. 'There was such a lot of cooking to be done and so much food to be stored. Mr Nairn saw the need to bring in modern equipment to help me deal with it all. There was also a temporary woman engaged to help me. Much needed, I can tell you.' Mrs Peterson shook her head, remembering sometimes there was such a large crowd of noisy, hungry men. 'It was hard work, I can tell you. I was always glad when he was away abroad on shooting parties.'

Jessica decided not to speak about the hotel plan until she'd spoken more about it with Brian. She'd then be able to assure Mrs Peterson that there would be many more staff than just one temporary woman.

Jessica now sincerely appreciated Mrs Peterson and her obvious cooking talents and so did the twins. They thoroughly enjoyed the tasty tea and cakes Mrs Peterson always had ready for them after they arrived home from school. Then later at six o'clock, they all enjoyed a delicious dinner. Jessica was sure Brian would appreciate Mrs Peterson's talents too and she longed for his return more and more each day. She was happy, though, collecting information and getting to know everything about the history of the area, which she was sure would add to Brian's interest and enjoyment. She felt a thrill of excitement at how proud she could imagine he would be of her. (She was even beginning to think of writing pamphlets about the area to distribute to hotel guests.)

'You were a wonderful tourist guide for me in Glasgow, darling,' she could hear Brian saying. 'Now you're going to be an equally wonderful guide for the Campsie area. How on earth do you manage it?'

She missed Brian. She missed everything about him but especially his passionate love-making. It occurred to her then that it would be better to arrange for a couple of smaller beds for Fiona and Tommy while Brian was in the big bed with her. They could be put in another room but she felt it would be cruelty to banish them to one of the other huge rooms on their own.

She had a talk with Mrs Peterson about the beds and Mrs Peterson said it would be no problem.

'Don't worry, Mrs Anderson. There will be no problem in arranging that. We have several small old-fashioned truckle beds that can roll under the big bed during the day.'

Brian would also be delighted, Jessica was sure, about the improvements Patrick O'Rourke had already made on the grounds. She was interested to learn more about him too. There was much more to Patrick than just being a joker. She made a note to pass on to Brian a song she had heard Patrick sing to the children.

'The kiss of the sun for pardon.
The song of the birds for mirth.
One is nearer God's heart in a garden
Than anywhere else on earth.'

He had an obvious love of gardens and his work in them and there was a poetic side to his nature that she couldn't help admiring. She often heard him say things to the children like, 'Some flowers seem to smile; some have a sad expression.'

Some other remarks he made gave her pause for thought. 'The most beautiful things in the world: peacocks and lilies, for instance.'

One rainy day she heard him say,
'This is the weather the cuckoo likes

And so do I.
When showers betumble the chestnut spikes,
And nestlings fly.'
Everything said in his lovely Irish accent and often with his dimpled smile had begun to cast a spell over Jessica as well as the children. She now admired his talent for creating and reciting poetry as much as she admired his talent for gardening. One cold day, he told the children in a sad, gentle tone,
'The North wind doth blow,
And we shall have snow
And what will poor robin do then, poor thing?
He'll sit in a barn
And keep himself warm,
And hide his head under his wing, poor thing.'
Once when he remarked on her sad expression, he added,
'I go to nature to be soothed and healed, and to have my senses put in order.'
She could no longer regard him just as a pain in the neck and a silly flatterer, as she had at their first meeting. There was obviously much more to the man than that. All right, he could still be a bit of a joker but he had such an amazing artistic side to him and his artistry went far beyond his gardening talents. Actually she had become most grateful to him for making her laugh and also for interesting her and intriguing her with his poetry quotations. Once you got to know him, it became obvious that he was really a truly charming man.

She began to feel much better and more cheerful about everything. After all, she was very lucky having such a good staff already and soon there would be lots of other people on the staff and then the whole place would be busy and cheerful and interesting with lots of guests. People maybe coming from different parts of the world, not just from different parts of Scotland. She nearly drove herself mad with her impatience to get the whole business started. Especially when she got word from Brian that he'd be delayed for another week or two.

'I've told you before what the Saudis are like. They take ages before they even start to talk about business. They enquire about your health, your family and God alone knows what else. Their every relative under the sun comes to do the same. There are meals to take and gifts to accept. There are distractions and delays that go on and on. I'm so sorry, darling, but as soon as I arrive, we'll get cracking on all the arrangements for the hotel. Meantime, if you want to (knowing your impulsive nature), you can tell Mrs Peterson and discuss it with her. She's the one who no doubt would know about the best people to staff the place, etc.'

At least that was a relief and Mrs Peterson immediately warmed to the idea, probably infected to some degree by Jessica's enthusiasm and excitement. Even Geordie nodded his head and remarked that it was 'a bloody good idea' and that it was 'time something sensible was done with the place'.

Patrick had been out working in the grounds when she'd told the Petersons and she couldn't wait until he came in. Often he worked outside until just before their meal at six o'clock. And so, on her way down to collect the children from school, she sought him out and immediately on catching sight of his blond head, she rushed to tell him all about the plans. He too was delighted.

'Wonderful. Wonderful. And trust me, my lovely Jessica, I'll work like a slave to get the grounds at least in a decent state as quickly as possible. But I'll have to go on concentrating on the road just now and make it wide enough for cars, don't you think?'

'Oh definitely, Patrick, and I'm really most grateful for your conscientiousness. I must speak to Brian about a raise in your wages. You're obviously worth a lot more than we're paying you at the moment.'

'As far as I'm concerned, Jessica, it's not a question of money. I love my work and I love working for such a lovely lady as your dear self. I'm a lucky man. A very lucky man.'

He walked down with her to the village and after she had collected the children, he wheeled them back to the house in his barrow.

As they walked down and back again, they discussed lots of ideas and plans for having Hilltop House as a hotel.

'It has such character and atmosphere,' Patrick said. 'People will love it. It'll make a fortune as a hotel. You'll have to do something about getting a phone installed, though. There's a limit to how isolated people want to be.'

Jessica found the money-making side attractive. It could be, as Brian had said at the start, a very good investment. Very little would need to be done to the house itself, apart from getting a phone installed. It would be best to leave the house as it was, as much as possible, to keep its unusual character. So the house wouldn't take much time. The gardens and grounds were a different story.

'Patrick, I'm just thinking,' she said eventually. 'You'll need help. Can you find people in the village or advertise or whatever for men to help you? I know that won't be easy. Local men don't seem to want to work on the grounds here. But as you said, the road especially will have to be widened as quickly as possible. And think of the whole estate. You definitely need workers you can instruct on what to do in different areas. It's especially difficult with the ground being so hilly.'

'I didn't like to mention it before, Jessica, but in actual fact a landscape gardener is just supposed to design what's needed. I've always been just a designer until I came here. So yes, I'll try to find some working gardeners to get on with the job as quickly as possible.'

'Gosh, I feel terrible now for expecting you to do all that work.'

'No, I just wanted to please you, dear beautiful Jessica. It was my choice.'

'Will I advertise or will you? Maybe you should see to it, though, Patrick.'

'Yes, I'll see to it. There's no need for you to worry.'

He gave her one of his dimpled smiles and added, 'I know gardening requires lots of water, most of it in the form of perspiration.'

'Meantime, Patrick, just forget all about the work you've been doing for the children. They can make do with the sandpit and swings for a while. They don't need anything else.'

Thinking of the swings Patrick had erected for the twins reminded her of what he'd said to them about that.

'How do you like to go up in a swing,
Up in the air so blue?
Oh, I do think it the pleasantest thing
Ever a child can do!'

They happily returned with the children ready for their tea and cakes in the kitchen. They were not long seated, however, when there was a loud clanging of the front door bell. This was an unusual event and Mrs Peterson hurried away to answer the door. In a few minutes she returned white-faced.

'Mrs Anderson, there's Dr Plockton and Mr Brown waiting to speak to you. I've shown them into the sitting room.'

Jessica felt confused as she left the kitchen. It surely couldn't be anything to do with the children. They seemed perfectly well and happy.

Once she was in the sitting room, Dr Plockton said, 'As you know, there is no police station in Vale of Lennox or even in Lennoxtown, Mrs Anderson. And of course you've no phone here so the police in Kirkintilloch phoned me and I contacted Mr Brown in case you needed extra help and support, especially with the children. I know that you have a high regard, as everyone has, for . . .'

'Doctor,' Jessica interrupted in desperation, 'what on earth's wrong?'

Douglas Brown came across to her, took her arm and led her to a seat.

'I'm very sorry to have to tell you, Mrs Anderson, that your husband has been killed in an air crash. He was travelling from . . .'

But Jessica didn't hear any more.

22

Douglas Brown comforted the children and Dr Plockton gave Jessica a tranquilliser. Mrs Peterson brought them all a cup of tea. The clock in the sitting room tick-tocked loudly and mercilessly.

Jessica couldn't believe it. It was too terrible to take in. Her whole life, all her plans, everything had revolved around Brian. He was her first and only love. He had opened new worlds to her. He had enriched her life. He had given her two lovely children. She struggled to find comfort in them. She had always loved and cherished the children. Now she would cherish them even more.

They had been weeping in the school teacher's arms. But he had soothed away their tears. She did not know what he had said to cause them to stop sobbing but they were just clinging to him in silence. They looked calm and comforted. It was as if some of his quiet strength had gone into them.

After a time, Mrs Peterson entered the sitting room – after knocking respectfully at the door – and asked if Mr Brown and Dr Plockton would be staying for dinner. They rose then, thanked her but said no, they would be leaving shortly. Mrs Peterson withdrew and Dr Plockton said to Jessica,

'Take another tranquilliser after your meal and then the sleeping tablet later, once you're in bed. Come to see me tomorrow and we'll talk things through.'

Douglas Brown said, 'If I can help in any way, with the arrangements or anything else, please just let me know.'

Jessica rose too. 'Thank you both for your kindness. It was so good of you to walk all the way up here. I really appreciate it.'

After they had gone, she and the children went through to the kitchen.

'I'm so sorry, Mrs Anderson,' Mrs Peterson said.

Patrick O'Rourke came towards her and put his arms around her.

'My poor dear Jessica,' he said quietly.

'By God, we'll all have to watch him now,' Geordie growled.

Mrs Peterson tutted.

'What nonsense are you talking now, Geordie? Can't you see the poor woman's grieving and needing comforting?'

'You mark my words,' Geordie said.

Patrick led Jessica over to a chair at the table. 'Maybe a cup of tea before dinner, Mrs Peterson?'

'Yes, of course. And here's wee cans of Irn Bru for Tommy and Fiona. They've been so good and so brave, haven't you?'

The children accepted their drinks.

'Say thank you,' Jessica said automatically, and the children dutifully complied.

Mrs Peterson switched on the small, old-fashioned television set and they settled down to watch their favourite programme as they sipped at their drinks. They did this every evening and then played card games or other games with Patrick.

This evening, Patrick searched out a few books from the musty library. One was *Treasure Island*. Another was *Robinson Crusoe*. He announced that he was going to read to them instead. This he did after they had all had dinner, and when the children's eyes began to droop, he led them up to bed. Jessica followed.

'I thing I'll have an early night,' she told Patrick. 'Thank you for your help with the children.'

'Will you be taking them to school as usual tomorrow?'

'Oh yes. I'm sure that'll be for the best – to keep them to their usual routine. And Mr Brown is obviously so good with them.'

'Right. Until tomorrow then, dear Jessica.' His arms enfolded her again. 'My deepest sympathy.'

'Thank you.'

She closed the door behind him and leaned against it, struggling not to weep.

'Are you all right, Mummy?' Fiona asked worriedly.

'Yes dear. I'm fine. The pair of you cosy into bed and I'll be with you in a few minutes.'

Once in bed she put her arms around the children and prayed for sleep to come quickly and blot out all thoughts.

Thanks to Dr Plockton's tablets, it did come quickly, and even in the morning it took her a few minutes after opening her eyes to remember what had happened the night before.

Then a wave of panicky disbelief rushed at her. It was only the children getting up and chatting about the exciting things that Mr Brown had promised to give them at school that helped her capture some sort of normality. She clung to it to help her get up and get bathed and dressed and act normally.

She then began to realise that all sorts of arrangements had to be made and awful things had to be thought about. Where was Brian's body? Would there be a body after a plane crash? Did the plane crash into the sea? Would it be possible to have a funeral and if so, where would it be? Where could it be?

After she'd delivered the children to the schoolhouse, she confided in Douglas Brown and pleaded for his help. He seemed the only and most obvious one to help and advise her. Patrick O'Rourke, with his long blond hair tied back and his slim figure and blue eyes and dimples, neither looked dependable nor gave the impression of being dependable. (Apart from his work, of course.) He was warm and sympathetic but much more than sympathy was needed now. Douglas Brown was a solid and very practical man in comparison both in looks and in nature. He had dark eyes and a strong, steady stare. He was tall and broad-shouldered, with well-developed muscles. She discovered he was a black belt in karate and she had mentioned that the children had been learning karate in the compound. He had been very impressed and spoke of perhaps starting a karate club with the children in his care. They might enjoy it, he said, and it would be a good and useful skill for them all to have. He had started the club and she'd watched them enjoy it when she'd called to collect the children.

Now he settled all the children with some lessons and took her into the adjoining kitchen so that they could talk in private.

'Leave everything to me,' he told her. 'I'll make the necessary enquiries, find out what arrangements are necessary. Then we can discuss them and make them together, or I'll make them for you on my own, if necessary, to avoid any distress to you.'

'It's so kind of you,' she said weakly. 'So kind.'

'Not at all. I'd do the same for any of the mothers if they were on their own like you, and needing help. This is a small, close community and we always try to help one another.'

It was such a pity, Jessica thought, that Mrs Plockton took advantage of this wonderful community spirit. She was the reason that Jessica did not go first to Dr Plockton for help and advice.

True to his word, Douglas Brown made all the necessary enquiries and arrangements. The plane had gone on fire and crashed into the sea. No bodies had been found, but he arranged for a memorial service in the church on the Green, which was beautifully and sympathetically conducted by the local minister, the Reverend MacNeil.

Afterwards, they'd had a meal in the hotel on the Green. Mrs and Mrs Peterson were there, and Patrick O'Rourke,

Dr and Mrs Plockton and Douglas Brown, and two or three others. It was a small gathering because, of course, few people in the area knew Brian. A couple of the other mothers came for Jessica's sake because they'd met her and chatted with her when they were dropping off their children at school and collecting them at the end of the day.

Once the meal was over, Jessica thanked everyone and said her goodbyes. Then she and the children, the Petersons and Patrick O'Rourke set off on the road back to Hilltop House. Patrick put his arm around her waist for support and half-carried her. He'd offered to lift her up in his arms and carry her properly but she refused to allow him to do that. She secretly thought he didn't look all that strong and she had a vision of his lanky body collapsing under the weight of her long before they reached the house. But she told him she appreciated his kind offer but he should concentrate on helping the children.

Mrs Peterson made a pot of tea as soon as they all arrived back in the kitchen.

While they were sitting round the table sipping the hot comforting liquid, Mrs Peterson asked, 'Will you still be going ahead with the hotel idea?'

'Yes,' Jessica said. 'Definitely. It was what Brian wanted. He was so full of enthusiasm about it. For his sake, I must get it organised right away. Will you go ahead and see to the staffing, Mrs Peterson, and Patrick, you're going to see about gardeners, aren't you?'

'Everything's in hand, Jessica.'

'Fancy,' Jessica told Mrs Peterson. 'I didn't realise that a landscape gardener was a designer and I was expecting Patrick to do all the spade work and everything.'

'Oh, I see to ponds, pools and rockeries, steps and patios as well. I can turn my hand to anything.'

Geordie's mouth twisted.

'Aye, you're awfae good wi' women as well!'

Patrick's cheeks dimpled. 'Ah Geordie, you noticed. And I can't deny it. Like Robert Burns, I do love the fair sex.'

He turned to Jessica. 'I'm a fan of your national bard. Have you read much of his work, Jessica?'

'I know most of the famous ones.'

Patrick gazed at her and his beautiful Irish voice softly recited,

'O my love is like a red, red rose,

That's newly sprung in June.

O my love is like the melody

That's sweetly play'd in tune.'

Geordie spat into the fire and said, 'Aw shit.'

23

'Mummy,' Tommy said, 'Patrick doesn't play with us any more.'

'That's just because he's so busy now, dear. We're all busy with making this place into the hotel that Daddy wanted it to be. Patrick has all that road to widen and these big hilly grounds to see to. And he's to be there to tell the gardeners what to do and make sure they do it right.'

Fiona said, 'Did you get our karate suits yet?'

'Yes. Where's the parcel? Oh yes, here we are.'

Tommy and Fiona immediately pounced on the parcel and tore it open. Fiona said,

'They're great but where did our other karate suits go? Remember we had them in the compound?'

'I know, dear, but with all that rush getting away, I'm afraid we forgot to bring a lot of things. Anyway, I didn't think you'd need them in a wee country village where nothing would be going on.'

'Mr Brown has lots of great things going on,' Fiona hotly defended the teacher. 'Even in a wee country village, he has more going on than there was in the compound.'

This was such an exaggeration that it was an effort for Jessica not to smile.

'You're right, dear. He certainly is a wonderful teacher.'

He was a wonderful teacher, right enough, and he had also become a good and dependable friend to her.

For touching sympathy, however, there was Patrick. He would sometimes put his arms around her waist as they walked together over the grounds of the estate. He talked about all the plans in progress. Jessica spoke about Brian and what he would think of everything. Patrick showed her the small classical fountain set in a shallow circular pool. He also pointed out the pre-cast pool in a sloping part of the garden that had been cleverly camouflaged with plants. There was the man-made water feature incorporating cascades and pools with various water-loving plants, giving it a natural charm.

In another area there were Art Deco steps. She remarked about them, 'They seem to beckon you to climb them, don't they?'

Patrick squeezed her waist. 'It makes it all worthwhile when you appreciate it so much, Jessica.'

She smiled but delicately drew away from him.

'I love the new patio.'

'Yes, it's a crazy-paved circular one. It makes a good surface for bench seats and picnic tables. I thought it would be handy for hotel guests sitting and sunning themselves.' He smiled. 'That's if we're lucky enough to have a sunny summer. But lots of people will come to Hilltop House anyway, no matter what the weather is like. It's such a fascinating place, with such an unusual atmosphere.'

Sometimes the children walked up the road by themselves now because, as Patrick said, they knew the way and he and the gardener were always around somewhere nearby to look out for them. And after all, they were ten years old now. Soon they would have to travel a much longer distance to one of the big schools. It was good to give them this chance, Patrick said, to learn to be independent.

'And it's easier now that the road's wide enough for cars.'

In the struggle with her grief over losing Brian, Jessica appreciated Patrick's warm sympathy, although she also struggled not to go to the extremes that Brian had always warned her against. Now this meant trying to keep Patrick from going to any extremes either. It was to her, not the children, that he recited and quoted lovely poetry.

'I know not how it is with you –

I love the first and last

The whole field of the present view,

The whole flow of the past.'

One poem he had quoted about a deserted old shooting lodge made her cry out, 'Thank God at least Hilltop House isn't like that any more.'

There were still all the antlers and heads and skins of animals that were the result of Mr Nairn's shooting parties. At first, Brian had agreed that they should be taken down and destroyed, and perhaps nice paintings hung to replace them. But once they'd decided to have the place as a hotel, he'd changed his mind.

'I think we should keep the hall as it is until we get a response from guests. If most guests don't like the look of the walls, then we can strip all the heads and skins, and so on, and replace them with paintings. Until then, I think we should leave the hall, like everything else, as it is.'

But they were not going to have any more shooting parties, of course.

Jessica kept herself busy with the preparations for the hotel and only saw Patrick occasionally during the day and in the evening, but once she was taken aback in the garden with him grabbing her hand and swinging her along as he sang,

'And it's westering home and a song in the air,

Light in the eye, and it's goodbye to care.

Laughter o' love and a welcoming there,

Isle of my heart, my own one.'

She couldn't help smiling. He really was a remarkable and endearing man. She was getting quite fond of him.

* * *

Tommy and Fiona didn't like Patrick any more. They hardly ever saw their mother. She was so busy doing things in the house and discussing things with Mrs Peterson. When they did see her, Patrick was always there. It was the only time he was in the slightest way pleasant to them. At any other time, if they saw him when their mother wasn't there, he was dismissive and unpleasant. They were becoming frightened of him. They instinctively felt he was up to something but they didn't know what. Until, that is, they overheard a conversation between him and Geordie. They had been on their way to watch them working on the road. It was when they were walking along behind some high bushes that they heard Geordie say,

'Aye, you're fairly getting your feet under the table now, eh? You've got that poor lassie eating out of your hand.'

They heard Patrick's laughter. But it wasn't a nice laugh.

'Once I get a ring on her finger and I own this place, you and your missus had better look out. Do you understand?'

'Oh aye, I've understood you right from the word go, you rotten two-faced swine. You'll be the death of that poor lassie yet.'

Tommy and Fiona stood frozen in horror. They very quietly sank down on to their knees to remain hidden until both Geordie and Patrick moved away. Then they scrambled up and ran back to the house.

Once in the house, they couldn't find their mother and had to ask Mrs Peterson where she was. 'Your mother was looking for you,' Mrs Peterson said. 'She's had to go to Glasgow for bed linen and towels and things. She'll be back tonight.'

Tommy blurted out, 'We wanted to tell Mummy that Patrick's a bad man.'

'Oh yes, we live and learn. We know that now, son. Sit down and don't you worry your heads about that rascal. Here's a couple of Irn Brus.'

Both children were taken aback by Mrs Peterson's attitude. How could she remain so calm? 'We,' she'd said. Did that mean she and Geordie knew that Patrick was a bad man or did it mean their mother knew as well?

'Does Mummy know that he's a bad man?'

'Oh, don't worry, she'll know soon enough.'

What did that mean? How could she find out?

Because it was the start of the school summer holidays, the day stretched long and dangerously before them. After a frightened whispered conversation, they decided to leave a note for their mother telling her what Geordie and Patrick had said and then they would go down and tell Mr Brown and feel safe with him. He would know what to do to protect them and their mother.

They wrote the note, put it in an envelope and addressed it: 'To Mummy, from Tommy and Fiona. URGENT.'

Then they propped it up on the kitchen table. They had been going to give it to Mrs Peterson to pass on to their mother but Mrs Peterson was nowhere to be seen and they were desperate to get away before Patrick appeared in the house. He would guess by their guilty, frightened appearance that they'd found out about him.

They ran from the house and out on to the hilly slopes of the garden. They prayed that Patrick would not be on or near the path. Their prayers were not answered because they heard the sound of running feet and turned to find Patrick running down the path towards them. In no time, he'd caught up with them and grabbed them both by the scruff of the neck.

'You little bastards. If you write any more notes or speak to your mother or anyone else in a bad way about me, I'll kill you. Do you hear me? I'll kill you and your mother.' He pushed his face near to theirs. 'I'll know. I'll find out, as I've found out today. I'll stab a knife into your precious mother and I'll make you watch me cutting her up into pieces before I start on the pair of you. Do you understand?'

In absolute terror, they nodded their heads.

'I promise you that's what I'll do. Never you forget it. Now get back to the house.'

He caught them by the hair and cracked their heads together. In physical agony now, they did as they were told and staggered back towards the house.

24

Jessica was late in returning from Glasgow and because the children looked so pale and drawn, Mrs Peterson had put them to bed early. Despite their distress, they fell asleep almost immediately.

Jessica checked that they were all right and gave their sleepy faces a kiss before she returned downstairs.

'As well as all the shopping, I took the chance of having a look around the Barras and visiting my friend Evie,' she told Mrs Peterson. 'And I'd some business with the solicitor as well, so I got a lot done. I hope you didn't have any bother with the children.'

'No, no. They looked extra tired, that was all, so I thought it best to put them to bed early.'

Geordie came in then with a pail of coal, raked out the fire and built it up with fresh coal. Then he disappeared to empty the ash pan outside. After he returned, he sat down at the table beside them, lit his pipe and said,

'Had a good day?'

'Yes, I was just telling Mrs Peterson. I got a lot done. I visited the Barras and a friend in the Calton, as well as shopping. I enjoyed seeing some old friends again. Where's Patrick, by the way?'

Mrs Peterson said, 'I think he and some of the men were putting some last touches to the road. There's a lot more to do to make it attractive, he says, but at least a car can get up it now.'

'I thought that as I was coming up tonight. I was glad of my trolley to carry my shopping. But I was just thinking – next time I could get a taxi up. I didn't see Patrick or the men, though.'

'They must have moved to another part. He's really keen to get everything looking its best in time to make a success of the hotel. It won't be long before you can advertise and give a definite date, will it?'

'No. It depends on how many staff you can get, Mrs Peterson. How are you doing with that?'

'Oh, I've had quite a few accepted jobs already. They're fine when they realise it's not going to be so isolated. I mean the road being opened up, and so on. And of course I was able to tell them that the phone people are due to come any time now and get all the phones installed.'

'So we can plan for an opening date in say a month's time at most?'

'Definitely.'

'I'll try to make it earlier because of the school holidays. Some folk would maybe want to bring their children.'

Mrs Peterson said, 'I think the twins are missing school already. They didn't seem to know what to do with themselves today.'

'Missing Mr Brown more than anything, probably. They're very fond of him. Has he gone away on holiday somewhere?'

'He's got a caravan up in Wester Ross. He often goes there for a week or more during the summer. I hear it's a really beautiful area.'

'I feel guilty at not giving so much time and attention to the twins just now, especially when they've no school to go to and fill up their days.'

'It's just temporary and you've no choice. There's so much to do at this early stage. But once the hotel is up and running, it'll be different. And the children have lots they can do. There's the swings to play on for a start, although they're a bit big for the sandpit now.'

'Yes, that was good of Patrick to do that for the children.'

Geordie spat in the fire. 'There's method to his madness. You mark my words.'

Mrs Peterson looked uncomfortable. 'Best just mind your own business, Geordie.'

'Best for who?'

Just then Patrick came into the kitchen and went over to the sink to wash his hands.

'Dear Jessica, it's so good to see you. Everybody misses you when you go away and nobody misses you more than me.'

Jessica smiled. 'I was so glad to see the progress you've made on the road. What a difference it'll be now that cars can get up and down.' She sighed. 'If only Brian could see how we're getting on. He was so keen on the idea of Hilltop House being transformed into a successful hotel.'

'Aye,' Geordie said, 'he'd be pleased about how you're getting on with the hotel but no' how you're getting on wi' him.' He cocked a thumb in Patrick's direction.

'How do you mean?' Jessica said worriedly.

Patrick laughed. 'Don't listen to him. He's just jealous. And how was your day, my lovely girl?'

Relaxing again, Jessica said, 'I was just telling Geordie and Mrs Peterson how I got quite a lot of shopping done today but I was able to visit my old stamping ground at the Barras market as well. It was great seeing everyone again. But it made me realise that this is my home now. This is what Brian wanted and so this is where my heart is now.'

'Aye,' Geordie said. 'Don't you forget your good man.'

'Geordie,' his wife cried out in embarrassment. 'Mind your place!'

'Don't worry, Geordie,' Jessica said. 'I'll never forget Brian. He opened so many new and fascinating worlds for me. Saudi Arabia, for instance. You've no idea what a different world that is. Really fascinating. Then he introduced me to this world. Hilltop House is equally fascinating in its own way. Brian could see it would make a great investment as a hotel and I believe he was right again.'

Mrs Peterson got up.

'We've had our dinner, Mrs Anderson, but there's plenty left if you feel able for something.'

'Just a cup of tea and a sandwich, please. Then I'll have an early night. There's lots to do tomorrow again.'

'I knew you wouldn't manage all the linen in one go.'

'It's a pity we couldn't use what was already on all the beds but it was pretty tatty, wasn't it?'

'I was ashamed of it long ago but Mr Nairn wouldn't lay out any money on that sort of thing. He used to say that most of the shooters would be so drunk by night time they wouldn't know what was on the beds. He was right enough because sometimes there weren't enough sheets to go around but nobody noticed. They just slept between the blankets.'

'Well, nobody will need to do that now. But as you say, I didn't manage it all in one go. Tomorrow I'll fetch the rest and the towels and table covers. Will you be all right with the children again?'

'Yes, of course. They're no bother.'

Patrick came over and sat beside Jessica.

'I'd love to show you what improvements we've managed today. Could you indulge me – give me half an hour of your time? It makes all the hard work so worthwhile. It is hard work, you know, dear Jessica. I give so much of my time from early morning till late every night.'

'Oh, of course,' Jessica said guiltily. 'I'll come right now, Patrick. I do appreciate all the extra hours you put in.'

She got up and hastily pulled on her jacket. Patrick indicated for her to precede him through the door and so she didn't see the triumphant look he flashed at Geordie and Mrs Peterson before he followed her outside.

It was a still, warm evening. No trees rustled or flowers nodded. Patrick put an arm around her waist.

'I'm so glad you said your heart was here now, Jessica. Our hearts are here together.

> And on that cheek, and o'er that brow,
> So soft, so calm, yet eloquent,
> The smiles that win, the tints that glow,
> But tell of days in goodness spent,
> A mind at peace with all below,
> A heart whose love is innocent!

Jessica smiled. 'Where do you get all your poetry? You don't just make it up, do you?'

Patrick rolled his eyes. 'I've been found out. You've seen through me. You're right. It's just that I'm fond of poetry and I've got a good memory for it.'

'I'm glad. It's always lovely to listen to. And I feel in a way there's a kind of poetry in your gardening too. It's certainly beautifully creative.'

'Thank you, Jessica. Certainly a lot of imagination is needed in gardening. Roses, for instance, are part of the summer scene and they're beautiful but can have even more impact when used with imagination.'

'Everything is so colourful – the wallflowers and, what are these?'

'Pelargoniums, popularly known as bedding geraniums. I like mixtures like those over there – wallflowers and forget-me-nots. And marigolds are always cheerful. As you can see, I also like plenty of clematis.'

All the time, as they walked along, he kept his arm around her waist. She felt she ought to untangle herself, push him away, but the warmth of him was so pleasant. What worried her was the stirring of sexual feelings she was beginning to experience. A throbbing inside her was giving her secret guilty pleasure.

25

There turned out to be much more shopping that Jessica had to do. Then there was the job of helping Mrs Peterson make up all the beds and put new cushion covers on a huge number of cushions. The whole place also needed to be vacuumed and thoroughly cleaned. As a result of all that work and more, Jessica hardly ever saw the children. Geordie was kept busy washing innumerable windows. The stairs were difficult but Mrs Peterson and Jessica managed between them.

At night, Jessica was so tired that she was glad to go to bed early. She sometimes just saw the children as Mrs Peterson was putting them to bed. Occasionally she was home in time to have the evening meal with them. She noticed that they were very quiet. There was no chatter now, there were no questions asked and there was no news delivered of what they had been doing all day.

Jessica took it for granted that they were just too exhausted. She was too exhausted too, but usually she was persuaded to go out for a walk in the grounds with Patrick, so that he could show her how the work was progressing. She was also persuaded because he spoke so interestingly about landscape gardeners of the past, like 'Capability' Brown. Capability Brown had apparently set up on his own, advising on estates across the country. Then he would brilliantly offer a whole package

– the technical survey and detailed plans, subcontracting and supervising the actual work, which could amount to thousands of man-hours of digging, building and planting. His fees were enormous because his clients were the top aristocracy. He was also gardener to George III at Hampton Court and imposed his will on the King by refusing for once to tear down the old avenues.

Someone once said to him, 'I very earnestly wish I may die before you do, Mr Brown.'

'Why so?' asked Brown.

'Because I would like to see Heaven before you have improved it.'

Jessica was fascinated by all of Patrick's stories. So much so that she forgot to push him gently away when he put his arm around her waist and held her close.

'Wisteria sisensis,' he was saying now. 'Such a beautiful Chinese plant and it has such a divine smell, don't you think?'

She did, and closed her eyes, savouring the heady scent of the beautiful purple plant. It was then that she felt Patrick's lips caress hers. Hastily she drew back from him and pushed his body away from hers.

'Patrick, please. I can't and won't come out with you again if you distress me like this.'

'Oh my love, I would never want to distress you in any way, ever. I thought our feelings were mutual. Please, please, forgive me.'

Jessica took deep breaths.

'I admire you and am fond of you as a friend, Patrick, but I'm still grieving for my husband. You must remember that.'

'In future, I'll try very hard not to express my deep and sincere love for you, Jessica.'

'Oh Patrick, you mustn't talk in terms of love.'

'Surely, at least, you won't deny me the pleasure of reciting my poetry. You said that you enjoy it. He smiled tenderly down at her.

'Had I the heavens' embroidered cloths,
Enwrought with golden and silver light,
The blue and the dim and the dark cloths
Of night and light and the half-light,
I would spread the cloths under your feet:
But I, being poor, have only my dreams;
I have spread my dreams under your feet;
Tread softly because you tread on my dreams.'

She could have wept. She needed someone to love her and Patrick was so loving and tender and sincere. But her need made her feel guilty. It was a sexual need Patrick aroused in her, not love. Her heart and mind still centred on Brian, especially when every minute of every day was filled with her efforts to fulfil his dream. He dreamed of having Hilltop House made into a successful hotel and she was going to do that for him.

'I want to go back to the house,' she told Patrick. 'Now.'

'Of course, my dearest beautiful Jessica. I'll take you back to the house now.' He left her outside the kitchen door, saying that he had to check on something before coming in.

Mrs Peterson had put the children to bed.

'I read them a couple of stories,' she said, 'and they settled down no problem.'

'You look upset,' Geordie growled. 'What's that Irish bastard been up to?'

'I'm all right, Geordie. But I appreciate your concern. By the way, when I was at the solicitor's, I told him to arrange for you and Mrs Peterson to be given a considerable raise in both your salaries.'

Mrs Peterson said, 'That's very good of you, Mrs Anderson, and it's much appreciated.'

'Aye,' Geordie agreed. 'That old skinflint Nairn would never have thought of that. You're a good wee lassie. Hard-working as well.'

'Thank you, Geordie. I'll have to go back to Glasgow tomorrow again to see him and check some other things that have occurred to me, as well as to do the rest of the shopping. You made me a list, didn't you, Mrs Peterson?'

'Yes, I have it here.'

They had a cup of tea and watched the news on television before Jessica decided to go upstairs to bed.

'Breakfast early again?' Mrs Peterson asked.

'Yes, thanks. See you then. Goodnight to you both.'

'Goodnight,' they replied and she left the kitchen, went through the dark, animal-lined hallway and climbed the stairs. Her mind and body were in turmoil. Seeing so much of Patrick in the evenings was not doing her peace of mind or body any good. She must try to be strong and refuse to go walking with him. At the same time, she felt bereft at the thought. Being with him and listening to his unusual conversation was so interesting. No, more than that – it was fascinating. She had never in her life heard anyone speak as he did. Certainly no one had ever spoken to her in such poetic terms. But she mustn't forget what all his soft talk could lead to.

Next day she collected her trolley and walked down to the village. There, to her surprise, she bumped into Douglas Brown.

'I thought you'd be away up north on holiday.'

'No. Perhaps nearer the end of the school holidays, I may go up for a few days, but just now I want to keep the karate class going. They enjoy it so much. By the way, I see the road's OK now but you haven't got the phone in yet.'

'No, but any day now, we hope.'

'I'm sorry the twins haven't managed recently. I'll drive up and collect them, if that's OK.'

'Wonderful. I've been away so much and have been so busy with hotel business, I'm afraid I've been neglecting them.'

'Fine. I'll collect them tomorrow then. Say about half past ten?'

'Yes, that'll be great.'

When she returned to Hilltop House, the twins were sitting at the table with Patrick and Geordie, and Mrs Peterson was dishing up the dinner.

'Just in time,' Mrs Peterson said as she dished up a bowl of home-made soup to Jessica.

'You'll never guess what,' Jessica told the children. 'Mr Brown is calling for you tomorrow after breakfast and driving you back down to the school to the karate class.'

The children's faces lit up slightly but they didn't show the wild delight she'd expected as a response.

'Is that OK?'

They both nodded.

Jessica wondered at the restraint they had been showing recently. Was it boredom or what? No doubt the action in the karate club would cheer them up and liven them up again. She sincerely hoped so anyway.

Later, when she'd gone upstairs with Mrs Peterson to put some cushion covers on and Geordie had gone out to fill a pail of coal for the fire, Patrick said to the twins,

'Now you two, remember – if you say anything to Mr Brown, *I'll know*, and I'll hack your mother to pieces. I'll cut her arms and legs off, and her head, and I'll show them to you as soon as you get back.'

The children's faces turned a sickly shade of grey and their eyes stretched enormous.

'Do you hear me?'

They both nodded.

'Right, now get up to bed out of my sight. But don't for one minute forget what I've said. Your mother's life depends on you keeping your mouths shut.'

Trembling, the children rose and, clinging to each other, they did as they were told.

26

The twelve pupils lined up in the schoolroom. All twelve were wearing their loose white karate suits. Mr Brown had previously given them a talk about karate and a demonstration and now they were about to begin their practice.

The work tables and chairs had been pushed to the back and the dozen young pupils lined up ready to begin.

Jessica waited for a few minutes at the outside door to watch the session. She saw Mr Brown pull the soft white jacket of his karategi over his thickly muscled shoulders, his body testament to years of working out.

Quickly he wrapped his tattered black belt around his waist and gave a brief bow before stepping into the gym, or as it was now temporarily designated, the Dojo.

The children were rushing around laughing and shouting, climbing on the wall bars and generally behaving as groups of children do.

Mr Brown clapped his hands together loudly and called out, 'Right, guys, let's line out.'

With much giggling and shuffling, they formed a rough line.

'OK, boys and girls. When I say the command "seiza", I want you all to kneel, then I say "sensei nel rei" and we all bow together. That means we are leaving our outside lives behind and training seriously. Any questions?'

'Yes sir. I thought you were a black belt, but that's all sort of white and grey and black.'

'Yes, that's right, Ian. That's because it's very old. It shows I've been a black belt for a long time now. I'm what's called a "third dan".'

The class started with ten minutes of stretching and warming up before Mr Brown started to teach the basic karate moves – how to stand, how to move and the basic blocks and strikes.

All things considered, it went well. He managed to keep a degree of structure and discipline while keeping it suitably light-hearted for a young group of beginners. Time enough to slowly build up the strict regime needed for success in the martial arts.

Afterwards, Jessica hurried away with her trolley to catch the bus to Glasgow. One of her ambitions was to learn to drive and get a car once she had the hotel up and running. It would transform her life and save such a lot of walking, not to mention time.

Once in Glasgow, she couldn't resist visiting the Calton area and of course the Barras market.

'We fairly miss Mrs Mellors,' one stall holder said. 'OK, her stall's being well looked after but the knitting's not as good as hers was. The stock she left is done now. I hope she comes back as promised. Three months, she said.'

'Yes. I eventually got her letter telling me she was going. It was held up for ages in Saudi. I haven't written to her about Brian's death or anything, so as not to worry her and spoil the lovely time I'm sure she'll be having with her family. She dotes on that son of hers. He's always been so good to her.'

After chatting for a time to different stall holders and old friends at the market, she went to visit Evie in the drop-in centre. It was while she was walking through the crowded streets that she realised that what she'd said recently was really true – her heart was not here any more. Her heart was in the wild and beautiful countryside of the Campsie Hills.

The problem there was Patrick O'Rourke. Some people might say he was a unique character and absolutely perfect. Not only was he good-looking and charming and so unusual in his poetic way of expressing himself verbally, but he was a wonderful, knowledgeable, conscientious worker as well. Why, anyone might ask, was she resisting him? She wasn't sure herself except that perhaps he was rushing her. She feared being dangerously swept away in an orgy of sex because that was what she experienced for him – sexual feelings. She somehow couldn't feel love for him, feel safe with him, trust him – and she had loved and trusted Brian.

It was lovely to listen to him reciting poetry but there was an unreality about the way Patrick spoke. It was as if he was acting all the time.

She needed reality. She needed Brian.

After a quick snack with Evie, Jessica travelled to the centre of town to the solicitor's office. Then shopping, then the bus back to Vale of Lennox. By the time she reached Hilltop House, the children were in bed sleeping and Patrick was nowhere to be seen.

Mrs Peterson persuaded Jessica to have a bowl of soup and a cup of tea, and she and Geordie sat chatting with her.

'I had quite a lot to get sorted out at the solicitor's,' Jessica told them.

Mrs Peterson said, 'I thought it was all arranged and provided for long ago. I mean, expenses and wages and all that.'

'Yes, that was already all in place. This was something different altogether. You see, I discovered that Brian didn't leave the property and the estate to me. He left everything to Tommy.'

'What?' both Geordie and Mrs Peterson cried out incredulously.

'Oh, Brian left me well provided for, don't worry. But it's perfectly understandable he'd leave the property and the estate to his only son.'

'Well,' Geordie said, 'I'll be buggered.'

'I had to check about how much authority I have to make decisions about the place, and so on, until Tommy is of legal age to make them himself.'

'And did you get it all sorted?'

'Yes. It's a bit complicated but it's OK. We can go ahead with all the arrangements exactly as we planned.'

Jessica and Mrs Peterson began talking about their plans for the next day. They were going to check through all the rooms to make sure that there was a little radio on each bedside table, a Bible in each bedside drawer, water jugs and glasses in every room.

Next day, Jessica kissed the twins before going upstairs and told them to have good fun playing in the garden. But she couldn't help adding,

'Are you all right? You're not too tired or anything?'

They shook their heads.

It was unusual for them not to chat and be eager and active, and Jessica felt worried.

'Are you sure you're all right?'

They both nodded and reluctantly Jessica accompanied Mrs Peterson upstairs and started, notebook in hand, to check all the rooms and note down what was still needed.

Geordie went outside and propped a ladder against one of the walls to continue with his window-cleaning. It was while he was up the ladder that he caught sight of Patrick and called him over.

'What's up with you?' Patrick said. 'I'm busy.'

'So am I, but I thought you'd be interested in the latest news.'

'What news?'

'Oh aye, very interested.'

'Spit it out, for God's sake. I told you, I'm busy.'

'Well, you know how you plan to get a ring on Mrs Anderson's finger, get hitched to her so that you can be boss of all that she owns?'

'So what? That's not news.'

'I know.'

Patrick turned to move impatiently away.

'Go to hell.'

'She doesn't own anything. That's the news.'

Patrick stopped. 'What do you mean? Of course she owns everything. Her husband owned everything and now that he's kicked the bucket, it has to go to her.'

'No, it hasn't.' Geordie was obviously enjoying himself.

'Stop messing about, you old fool. How can it not have gone to her?'

'Because . . .' Geordie paused for effect, 'her husband left the house and the estate to his son. That's wee Tommy.'

'Christ! I'll kill the useless wee sod.'

'Yes, everything belongs to wee Tommy and it's only if something happens to him that it would go to his mammy.' In sudden anxiety, Geordie added, 'But don't you get any ideas, you rotten two-faced swine. Nothing bad had better happen to that wee lad, do you hear me?'

But Patrick O'Rourke had gone, striding – almost running – away to disappear into the thick growth of the garden.

Tommy and Fiona watched him from where they were crouching behind a bush. They had heard every word of the conversation between Patrick and Geordie and now a new terror engulfed them.

There was no way that Patrick would take a telling from Geordie. He would kill Tommy. That's what he said and that's what he'd do.

The two children clung tightly to each other, sobbing quietly.

Then they whispered to each other about what they could do to keep safe. Eventually they decided to take the risk of leaving a note for their mother telling her that Patrick was going to kill Tommy and they were going down to the village to get Mr Brown to help them and keep them safe.

This time, they left the note in the bedroom to avoid any risk of Patrick finding it. Then they crept away over the other side of the hill. Once at the foot of the hill, they planned to walk round to the village. It was a much longer way than going down the road or any part of the front area of the garden. But it would mean that neither Patrick nor any of his gardeners would see them.

They'd never been down the other side of the hill before. There was the back garden first, and then there were trees and a drystone dyke, as it was known locally. Or in English, a drystone wall. The twins reached the wall and managed to climb over it, then they set off very nervously down the steep incline.

Back at the house, Patrick had returned to seek out Jessica and tell her that he'd just heard her news about the will and how delighted he was and how they must both treasure the dear wee soul and look after him until he was able to look after himself. Then he'd recite some poem about the love of children. He was trying to think up the best poem to melt her heart and influence her mind when he reached her bedroom and saw the note.

He read it.

27

The hillside was very steep and, in parts, rocky too. It made the twins feel dizzy as they hurried down, trying not to run but unable to stop themselves because of the steepness of the terrain. Then suddenly a tiny cottage came into view. It had only one shuttered window and a thatched roof. They managed to reach it and cling on to the wall, and then the doorway of the cottage for shelter from the wind that was now howling about in every direction.

An old woman lived in the cottage. Many years ago, so the story in the village went, her two children had been killed falling down one of the gullies. But she kept insisting to everyone that they'd come back to her. Now the cottage door opened and there she was, bent and frail-looking, with a shawl wrapped round her shoulders. On seeing the children, her face lit up with joy.

'I knew you'd come back,' she cried. 'I knew I hadn't lost you.'

She caught them into her arms and pulled them into the house. The twins were too surprised at first to make any objections.

'I'll pour you out a cup of milk and get your favourite biscuits.'

As soon as the old lady went over to a cupboard, the twins got to the door. She immediately drew them back again, but not before they'd caught sight of Patrick O'Rourke racing down the hill towards the cottage. He must have seen them, perhaps from one of the high Hilltop House windows, climbing over the wall and running down the hill. In a few minutes he would have reached the cottage.

They both burst into helpless tears.

'What's wrong, my wee lovies?' the old lady asked.

Tommy said, 'There's a bad man coming down the hill and he's going to kill me.'

'No, don't worry. I won't let him. I'm not going to lose you again. No, never.'

'But he'll have seen us come in here. He'll come in after us.'

'He won't find you in here. Don't worry, you can hide.'

Their weeping intensified with frustration. As far as they could see, it was only a tiny one-roomed place.

'Where can we hide?'

The old lady smiled. 'I said there was no need to worry, my wee lovies.' She pointed upwards. 'See, there's a wee loft. See that pole over in the corner? That pulls the loft door down. But first you're going to enjoy your favourite biscuits. I knew I'd be able to give them to you again. I always knew it.'

Before the children could run over to grab the pole, the door opened. Patrick O'Rourke stood in the doorway, holding up a big iron key.

'You're asking for trouble, you stupid old hag, leaving your key in the door.'

The old lady shuffled towards him.

'Give me my key and get out of here this minute.'

To the children's horror, O'Rourke felled the old woman with one terrible punch.

'Now,' he said to the children, 'I'm going to go out, lock the door behind me and put the key in my pocket so there's no chance of you getting the door open. There's no point in trying.'

He laughed. 'Then I'm going to set fire to the place and it'll be burned to a cinder. No one will ever know I've been here, or that you little scumbags have been in here either. The old hag's already a goner. Perfect. Just perfect.'

With one vicious swipe, he knocked the children to the ground. They lay dazed, unable to move. Until eventually they began to cough and choke. They struggled to their feet. Burning coal from the fire had been scattered over the floor and had set alight everything all around. They desperately tried to open the door, but O'Rourke had locked it. In desperation they managed to get the pole in the corner and pull down the loft ladder. They scrambled up into the cramped, low-roofed loft.

A sliver of light was coming in from a small roof window. On peering out, they saw the running figure of Patrick O'Rourke disappearing back up the hill. With great difficulty, they managed to squeeze out of the window and clutching at the jaggy thatch, they got down on to the mossy ground. From there they began running down towards the road to the village again and – they hoped – to the safety of the schoolhouse and Mr Brown.

They were absolutely exhausted by the time they reached their destination and had to sit in Mr Brown's kitchen for a few minutes before they were able to speak.

'Try to calm down. Take deep breaths,' Mr Brown told them. 'That's right. Take your time. You're all right now.'

It was Tommy who recovered first.

'When Patrick O'Rourke found out that my Daddy left Hilltop House and everything to me, he said he'd kill me.'

Then Fiona piped up, 'Geordie was there. He heard him say it.'

Tommy went on, 'And he really has been trying to kill me. And Fiona as well. He chased us to a cottage on the other side of the hill. He locked the door and put the key in his pocket and told us that we'd never get out. He knocked the old lady and us down and set fire to the place.'

Fiona said, 'We managed to climb out a wee roof window.'

Douglas Brown thought for a moment. Then he said,

'I'm going to make a phone call, and then I'm going to drive you up to Hilltop House.'

* * *

Not far away, Dr Plockton was sitting at his desk opposite a patient. A few minutes before the patient had arrived, he'd heard a scream and a thump. He'd gone through to the back stairs and found his mother lying unconscious at the foot of the stairs. He had hesitated, then turned away, shutting the door behind him.

He then sat attending to his patient, knowing that his mother could be dying without his help. Knowing that he should phone for an ambulance.

Now the patient was saying, 'I always feel better after seeing you and having a talk with you, Doctor. Everyone feels the same. We all know what a conscientious doctor you are and we can trust you.'

'Thank you,' Dr Plockton said. And with a sigh, he lifted the phone.

* * *

'Please don't take us back to Hilltop House. He'll be there,' the children cried out in terror at Mr Brown's suggestion.

'Don't worry. No harm will come to you,' he said. 'I'll be there at your side all the time. But we must confront him with your mother there – although she might not believe us. He'll just deny everything, you see.'

They saw, all right. Their mother had never believed anything bad about Patrick O'Rourke before. And so they were driven back up to Hilltop House. In the kitchen they found Patrick O'Rourke and Jessica.

156

'Where on earth have you been?' Jessica said. 'Patrick has been searching everywhere for you. It's very naughty of you to disappear like that.'

Tommy cried out, 'Patrick has been trying to kill me.'

Jessica sighed and shook her head.

'Don't talk nonsense, Tommy. Especially about somebody who's always been so kind and good to you.'

'It's not nonsense, Mummy. He chased me and Fiona into a cottage down on the other side of the hill and then set fire to it. But we escaped through a loft window and got to the schoolhouse. But he's burned the old lady to death in the cottage.'

Jessica turned to Douglas Brown.

'I'm sorry if you've been taken in by all this and had to drive all the way up here. The twins, especially Tommy, have always had a very vivid imagination, and I'm afraid recently, because of all the work in the house and the garden, I've been paying more attention to Patrick than to them. They've obviously been jealous. Patrick wouldn't hurt a fly.'

Douglas Brown said, 'I believe the children, Mrs Anderson, and I've phoned the police.'

'Oh no,' Jessica gasped. 'How could you, Mr Brown? On the word of two little children. Well, I can assure you, I'll back Patrick and I'll tell the police what a load of wicked nonsense all this is.' She turned to Patrick. 'I'm so sorry, Patrick.'

Patrick gave her one of his gentle, charming smiles.

'There's no need to worry. I forgive them.'

Jessica said, 'I'm really surprised at you, Mr Brown, believing the children's outrageous story without the slightest proof.'

Patrick said, 'I've never been near that cottage in my life. I've seen it in the distance from here but that's all.'

It was then that Fiona remembered and shouted out,

'The key. He put it in his pocket. The key of the cottage.'

Quick as a flash and before Patrick's hand even reached his pocket, Douglas Brown had pounced on him and snatched the old-fashioned key from him. Patrick turned to run but Douglas Brown felled him with only one karate kick.

It was only after the police had arrived and escorted the furious and vehemently cursing Patrick O'Rourke away that Jessica was able to speak. She stood holding the twins close to her and said to Douglas Brown,

'How can I ever thank you? You've saved my children's lives.'

Suddenly she burst into tears. 'How could I have been so foolish?'

Douglas Brown came over and his comforting arms enfolded her and the children.

'You're not foolish. You're a good and loving mother. O'Rourke can put on an unusually charming manner and I've no doubt the police will discover other people he's taken advantage of in the past.' He smiled. 'If it's any comfort to you, you've still got me. Charmless, no doubt, but at least you can trust me.'

'Oh Mr Brown . . .'

'Don't you think it's time you called me Douglas?'

'Yes, Douglas. And please call me Jessica.'

She managed to smile through her tears, especially when the children began jumping up and down with excitement and delight.

'Can we call you Douglas too?'

'Well,' he said smiling, 'perhaps Uncle Douglas.'

They clapped their hands now as they jumped up and down.

'Uncle Douglas. Uncle Douglas,' they sang out and Jessica couldn't help laughing.

It was then she realised that Douglas Brown's arms were still around her and she liked the strong, comforting feel of them. She said half to him and half to herself,

'I never thought I'd feel happy again.'

'Oh, you will from now on,' Douglas Brown assured her, and held her even closer.

If you enjoyed
DOUBLE DANGER,
don't miss these other
recent titles from
Margaret
Thomson
Davis

'one of Scotland's foremost novelists'

RED ALERT
By Margaret Thomson Davis

The compelling story of a Glasgow family torn apart by an abusive father.

Kirsty Price loves her job at the local fire station, especially when firefighter Greg McFarlane starts to pay her lots of attention. She's happy except for the fact that she's also the daughter of Simon Price, an artist and tutor at the Glasgow School of Art. He's a notorious bully, both to his students and his family, including Kirsty and her brother Johnny.

When Johnny accepts a job from a dubious couple who work as croupiers in the local casino, Kirsty starts to worry that all is not well. Then Greg phones to say that he has been attending a fatal road traffic accident and the car involved is Johnny's. The family is devastated but soon after Johnny's funeral, there's a knock at the door and Kirsty staggers back in shock when she sees who's standing in the shadows outside. But it's just the start of a chain of events that will tear the Price family apart and test Kirsty to the limit.

Available from

BLACK & WHITE PUBLISHING
www.blackandwhitepublishing.com

Price £6.99   ISBN 978 1 84502 246 4

GOODMANS
of
GLASSFORD STREET
By Margaret Thomson Davis

The story of a successful but old-fashioned family department store and the lives and conflicts of the people who work in it, including the strong-willed matriarch Abigail Goodman.

Douglas Benson, Abigail's son-in-law, is determined to gain control of the store and completely modernise it. He becomes more and more ruthless in his methods to oust Abigail but she is determined to hold on to the business and keep it as it is. She and her late husband, Tom, had taken over Goodmans of Glassford Street from Tom's father and built the business up together. All her memories are tied up with the store. They are all she has left of the happy life she and Tom shared.

As the struggle for control of the store escalates, Abigail's son John – an MSP who spends much of his time in Edinburgh – presents the family with another crisis. A serial killer is stalking the closes and wynds of the Royal Mile and it looks like John may be a suspect. It's a bitter blow to Abigail and the Goodman family at an already uncertain time.

Available from
BLACK & WHITE PUBLISHING
www.blackandwhitepublishing.com
Price £6.99 ISBN 978 1 84502 202 0